WITHIN DARKNESS

VOLUME ONE

AUDREY BRICE

AN ORDO TEMPLI SERPENTIS NOVELLA COLLECTION

WITHIN
DARKNESS

VOLUME ONE

AUDREY BRICE

AN ORDO TEMPLI SERPENTIS NOVELLA COLLECTION

Darkerwood Publishing Group
Colorado, U.S.A.

Darkerwood Publishing Group
Colorado, U.S.A.
First Paperback Printing, June 2016 - U.S.A.

ISBN: 978-1-938839-01-6

Dedication

For Marie

NOTE ABOUT THIS BOOK

Dear Reader, If you are not someone who is familiar with *real-world* occult practice, please know that my use of Magick, Daemon, and Daemonolatry etc... are not typos or spelling errors. I have purposefully chosen to spell these words as we do in real-world Daemonolatry. I do hope the gentle reader will forgive my non-traditional spellings and that it won't detract from your enjoyment of this book. Also, the rituals described within this book are real. Please be cautious and if you use them, do so at your own risk. Thank you – The Author.

Sunny Satan Arizona
OTS # 1.5
(Read between Outer Darkness and Into Darkness)

Mike scowled at the miles of desert we had to drive yet. Our destination remained my childhood home - Sandpiper Point, Arizona, a small town amid a desolate desert wasteland in the middle of nowhere. That alone was the biggest reason I moved to Colorado. When people asked, I often just told them I was from Tucson, or Phoenix if I was feeling brave. It was just easier than trying to explain Sandpiper Point. Sure, from Sandpiper Point one could drive an hour east and reach the suburbs of Tucson, or about two hours north for Phoenix, but that was beside the point. At least in Colorado there weren't scorpions or tarantulas or miles and miles of desert. Naturally my cousin Remy insisted on getting married in August, and my mother insisted I'd come.

Mike, feeling bad that I had to endure his overbearing mother, had consented to come with me. Thank gods it was only for a week.

My tall, dark-haired, gorgeous boyfriend pointed at a seemingly random saguaro cactus standing tall against the stark landscape, its arms lifting up into the sky. "Cool. Do they normally get that big?"

I couldn't tell if he was being smart or serious, and decided to treat it as an opportunity to wow him with a random fact. "They only grow in the Sonoran desert and they can grow up to seventy feet tall."

"Oh yeah?" His brown eyes didn't avert from the road.

Assuming it was a rhetorical question I didn't answer. Instead, I found myself getting increasingly nervous the closer we got. Would my parents like Mike? My mom in particular sounded eager to meet him and was tickled to death when I told her he was a detective. As she put it, it was about time I settled down with a *responsible* young man. Immersing myself in the task of checking my smart phone for messages I knew my family would want to spend some time with Mike and me. There was nothing else to do. Sandpiper Point was the epitome of small town life. There was one theater, one grocery store, one hardware store, one gas station, a diner, and a local newspaper ran by the owner of the gas station.

Newspaper is a bit strong actually. It's really more of a gossip newsletter where the news is everyone's personal business. I had no doubt that when we arrived I could pick up the local newsletter to see some kind of announcement about me and Mike's arrival.

We drove almost another hour through the desert before I had Mike turn off the highway and head toward my parents' house. I was glad we'd gotten a rental, because I certainly didn't want to put all that mileage on my car. Another half hour and we pulled up to the three bedroom ranch amidst the sprawling desert.

Mike parked the car off to the side of the garage and looked around, scratching at the five-o-clock shadow darkening his lower jaw. "Babe, you grew up here?"

He looked around at the barren landscape of scrub-brush, desert, and cacti.

I nodded. "Yep. Sunny Arizona!"

"Jesus Christ. It's hot."

"Yeah. Maybe we should move here…" I kidded.

"Hell no," he said. "This really is the middle of fuck nowhere, isn't it?"

From horizon to horizon there was nothing but sky, and desert as far as the eye could see. I unbuckled my seat belt and got out of the car. "Now you know why I moved."

Mike laughed and followed me to the front door. I still had a key and found myself relieved when it fit in the lock, turned, and opened the door easily. Neither of my parents' vehicles were out front so chances are they were in town or off doing something.

We went into the house and Mike seemed to relax when he realized there was AC. The pool looked inviting, too.

"We can go swimming later if you want."

"This won't be so bad," he said aloud, as if trying to convince himself.

I laughed. "As long as you don't mind sleeping on the sofa or the guest bed. My parents won't let us share the guest bedroom."

"I'll take the sofa," he said. "Tarantulas and scorpions?"

"Yeah, just empty out your shoes before you put them on. Oh, and sometimes lizards." I wandered through the dining room into the eat-in kitchen. "Of course my mom keeps the house pretty clean so bugs and lizards are a rarity in here. They do get in sometimes though."

Mike followed.

I saw the blue newsletter sitting on the kitchen table and immediately grabbed it. My eyes skimmed what bordered too much information until I found it. I read it aloud. "Elizabeth Tanner, daughter of Brian and Rachel Tanner of 442 Skyline Road, is coming home from Colorado for her cousin Remy's wedding this week, and bringing along her police detective boyfriend, Mike."

Mike smirked. "Nice."

"Oh, but things are going to be okay, because Joyce Merit's bunion surgery went well and she's currently recovering at her daughter, Viola's, house. Emmanuel Gutierrez finally finished restoring his 1952 Chevy and Rosa Murphy just delivered a healthy baby boy. Oh - and get this, little Annie Martinez just got a new puppy named Bruiser. I don't know about you, but I'm caught up." I tossed the newsletter back on the table.

He chuckled.

Just then the front door opened and my mom came through it carrying a grocery bag. "Elizabeth!" She made a b-line to the table, offloaded her groceries and embraced me in a huge hug. "Your dad is out at the car bringing in more groceries."

It had only been about a year since I'd been back, but I guess it was long enough. I returned the embrace. "Hi Mom."

Releasing me, she stepped back and looked Mike up and down. "You must be the Michael I've heard so much about."

Then she hugged Mike and the look of sheer terror on his face made me laugh. Mike, strangers, and hugging didn't go well together.

"So, where is Dad's pickup?" I asked.

"It's in the shop again. He really just needs to get a new truck," my mom said just as he walked in carrying more groceries.

Mike immediately moved to help him. "Here, let me help you with that Sir."

I followed my mom back out to the car. With the four of us, the groceries were in the house and unpacked in no time.

"So Mike," my dad said, "You ever play baseball?"

Oh gods, I'd forgotten my dad played baseball with his co-workers. They were probably one short.

"I've played before."

"Any good?"

"I've hit a home run or two in my day."

That seemed to be enough for my dad. I was right. "We play Thursday, but one of our guys sprained an ankle. You want to play this week?"

"Oh, uh," Mike looked at me, fumbling. "Uh sure."

My father led Mike away and he politely followed.

I shook my head.

My mom smiled, putting away the eggs. "He seems nice."

"He's actually *really* great." I admitted, catching a horrifying glimpse of my messed up auburn hair in the reflection of the microwave. Running my fingers through my hair, I straightened it up a bit. "I look like hell."

My mom ignored my comment. Evidently she had other things on her mind.

"Jerry Garza was asking about you last week. I told him you'd be here today. He said he would stop by, wanted to say hello." My mom gave me a wide smile. Every time I looked at her it was like looking in a mirror. We were both short and curvy, with the same high cheekbones and thin nose.

What was she up to? I narrowed my eyes. "Mom, why did you tell everyone I was going to be here?"

"Well, Elizabeth, people want to know. You have people here who love you."

"I know, but Jerry? You know he's been after me for years. You know I like him as a friend. I don't want Mike to feel unwelcome…"

"Well I don't know that his intention is to make Michael feel unwelcome." She looked toward the living room where the low cadence of men's voices chatted onward. "Jerry is a friend of yours and I'm sure Michael will understand if he wants to say hello. What's the harm in that?"

"Yeah, I guess you're right." I let out a sigh, trying to listen to what Mike and my dad were talking about. I couldn't catch anything.

"Now we have to go to your father's clients' house tonight for dinner so you and Michael will be on your own," my mother was saying. My father was a general contractor and constantly going to dinner at clients' houses.

"That's not a problem. We can go into town and have dinner at Max's." I careened my neck toward the living room. "I better go check on Mike."

"I'm sure he's fine. How was the drive?" my mother persisted.

"Long and hot. Kind of boring actually. We drove a rental." I nodded to the newsletter. "I'm all caught up with the town gossip."

"Indeed. You really shouldn't mock it. It's how we keep up with each other. Your big city life doesn't allow for that. Everyone is so disconnected."

"Well first, it's Denver, not New York City, and all of us suburbia people use social networking, which is kind of a bigger version of that," I said, pointing to the newsletter, "…

but you only have to tell your business to people you both know and like."

"Hmm, well, be nice to Jerry when he stops by." There was a hint of motherly warning in her voice.

"I'll be nice as long as he's polite to Mike." I knew Jerry well enough to know how he could be.

My mother got caught up putting her spices away so I used the opportunity to slip from the kitchen into the living room, worried that Mike would be upset that I didn't save him sooner. They were talking about football. Mike never really watched it at home, but he seemed to know a lot about it. Perhaps he just didn't watch it around me.

He appeared to be genuinely interested in my father, and my father him. So I let them be, grabbed me and Mike's suitcases that were sitting in the living room, and wandered back to the spare bedroom.

"Now Michael will be staying on the couch in the living room," my mother called out.

Oh good gods. I was a woman in my early thirties and she still treated me like I was sixteen. But my mom's house, her rules, and I knew she would be dead before she saw us sharing the same room under her roof if we weren't married. It was one of those bizarre religiously motivated social conventions I just didn't get.

"No problem, Mom. But I am keeping his suitcase in here so he has a place to change and it's out of the way," I called back.

"What if he has to get in there after you've gone to bed?"

"Good Lord, Mother, he's not going to molest me." *Because he already has*, I added silently with a snicker. I wandered back into the living room.

"Leave her alone, Rachel. Elizabeth and Michael are both adults," my dad chimed in.

WITHIN DARKNESS | AUDREY BRICE

"Well we don't need the neighbors talking."

My father shook his head. "The neighbors don't know what goes on in our house if we don't tell them, now do they?"

"Really, it's not a big thing. Mike will sleep on the couch, I'll sleep in the spare bedroom, and if he happens to need anything from his suitcase in the middle of the night, he promises not to molest me," I repeated.

"I solemnly swear," Mike said.

Fighting back a snarky laugh I sat down on the couch next to Mike. "Is it okay if I sit next to him on the couch?"

"Don't get cheeky with me, Elizabeth Tanner," my mother said, then went back into the kitchen.

My father laughed. "Remember that your mother's only social life is here in this town. She'd be mortified if everyone talked about you the way they talk about some of the girls you went to high school with. It was bad enough when she had to contend with those rumors about you being a witch."

I rolled my eyes. "Yeah."

Mike gave me a surprised look. "You were a witch?"

I laughed. "Long story. Maybe I'll tell you on the way to Max's Diner. That's where we're having dinner. The parental units have other obligations tonight."

"Yes, well, we'll have dinner with you kids tomorrow night," my father assured him.

The look on Mike's face said everything. I was going to owe him big time. Of course I'd contended with his mother plenty of times, so surely that would lessen my penance.

Just then a county sheriff's car pulled up in front of the house.

"Ah. Jerry Garza. He told your mother he was stopping by to see you," my father said, looking out the front window.

I got up and started toward the door. "Mike, come meet Jerry," I said, hoping to offer him a few minutes away from my parents. He got up and followed.

We stepped outside just as Jerry got out of his patrol car. He was still short and stocky, and still had a head of light brown hair, kept short and neat. The same smiling brown eyes.

Jerry and I had been close friends back in High School. I think he always wanted to date me, but he wasn't my type. Funny that he'd ended up working for the Pima County Sheriff's Department, especially since I'd ended up with a guy similar to him. Of course Mike was more progressive, forward thinking, and worldly than Jerry, and it was that progressiveness that made Mike and I *work*.

"Jerry!" I held out my arms and gave him a quick hug and said what everyone said when they saw someone they haven't seen in years: "Look at you! You look great!"

"You haven't changed one bit yourself," he said. "I keep missing you every time you're in town."

"I usually only fly in for a few days at a time." I motioned toward Mike. "This is my significant other, Michael."

Jerry looked Mike up and down, then reached out and shook his hand. "I always wondered who would land the elusive Elizabeth Tanner."

Land? What was I? A Cessna? A forced smile made its way, unbidden, across my face. *Be polite*, my civil self-scolded inwardly.

"She's not as elusive as you'd think," Mike said with cool detachment. "I only had to ask her out once."

Slam. I bit my inner lip to keep from laughing.

Jerry fought back an obvious frown and pushed a wayward strand of light brown hair from his eyes. The two-way radio he carried chirped and a tinny female voice came over the airwaves. I didn't catch what she said, except, "Five-nine-one respond."

He took up the radio and pressed a button. "Five-nine-one, go ahead."

"I need you to respond to six-twenty-three White Sands Drive. We have a ten-seventeen who claims there is an animal ritually sacrificed in their barn."

A look of concern passed over Jerry's face.

Jerry pressed the button again. "Is it like the others?"

"It appears so."

With a deep sigh, Jerry pushed the button again. "En route to ten-twenty."

"Animal sacrifice a big thing here?" Mike asked, his curiosity piqued.

"You're a big time detective, right?" Jerry asked, almost in a challenging way.

"I've worked my share of homicides. Of course in my cases the victims are usually human."

I braced myself, ready to foolishly jump in if Jerry and Mike started brawling. There was definitely tension between them, unless I was reading the situation wrong.

"You get a lot of Satanists in Denver?" Jerry gave me a sideways glance as he said it. He knew about my penchant for reading occult books when I was a teenager. Of course he didn't know it wasn't just a passing fad.

Mike shrugged. He couldn't really say no. In the past year he'd worked on more cases with an occult related link than he cared to admit. "Not really, but I've worked occult crimes before. That's how Liz and I met."

I thought my jaw would drop, but I held it steady, waiting for Jerry to respond.

"What would Liz have to do with that?" A sly grin grew on his lips.

"She knew some of the people we wanted to talk to and helped us get some information. That's all. She's rather well-read."

Inwardly, I breathed a sigh of relief.

Jerry looked at me for confirmation and I nodded. "I know some people who practice alternative religions."

"Satanists?"

"A few," I said. I wasn't lying. My best friend Alyssa was most certainly a Satanist. A perky non-stereotypical Satanist, but a Satanist nonetheless.

"Well maybe you two could be consultants on this case."

Mike was ready to jump on it, I could tell.

I, on the other hand, wanted to just go to my cousin's wedding and put this whole trip behind us. "Well, we have a lot of family things this week. Mike is playing baseball with my dad Thursday night, we're having dinner with my parents' tomorrow night, and then there's my cousin's wedding Saturday…"

"So you have a lot of free time," Jerry said, knowing better.

"Yeah, we do actually," Mike agreed.

Outnumbered, I let out an audible sigh. "I suppose we do. There really is nothing to do in this hell hole anyway except swim, eat and watch daytime television."

Jerry motioned to the car. "Hop in and come along."

"Hold on," I said, then darted into the house to grab my purse and my keys. "We're going with Jerry. We'll be back later, I have my phone."

"Don't be out too late," my mother said.

I felt like a teenager again. When I got back outside, Mike and Jerry were already in the car waiting for me. Guess who got to ride in the back like a criminal. Yeah, *this girl.*

While Mike and Jerry talked shop, I sat in the back looking out the window watching scrub brush, cacti, and small houses go by, all the while wishing we were back home in Colorado.

The farm we drove up on was quaint with that Southwestern appeal you only find in this part of the world. They even had old wagon wheels on either side of the driveway entrance. Jerry got out of the car first, followed by Mike, who opened the car door for me so I could get out. Outside a woman took a saddle off of a roan horse and set the saddle, pad and all, on the post rail fence the horse was tethered to.

"Junior, Deputy's here," she called toward the house. "He'll be with you in a moment Deputy."

"Thank you Marge," Jerry said. "Did you see it?"

"No, and I don't wanna. That's a mighty powerful curse to see something like that. Junior is gonna hafta call the pastor out to get rid of any demons," Marge said. Then she yelled at the house again, "Junior? You comin'?"

I half expected her to spit some chaw on the ground, and if this were Texas, she might have.

Mike and I exchanged glances and I clutched my purse, feeling horribly out of place.

A rough, unshaven guy with tattoos, mid-forties, stepped out of the house, sniffed, and rubbed his nose on his arm. He pulled a ball cap over his balding head of brown hair. "Who's them?"

Jerry nodded and motioned toward us. "Well this here is detective Katz from Denver, and his associate Ms. Elizabeth Tanner, an expert in the occult."

Never before had it been more apparent that I really came from country backwater and I wondered if acknowledging that made me a snob. I politely forced a smile.

"You know stuff about the o-ccult?" Junior asked, emphasizing the 'o'.

Mike bit his lip. I couldn't tell if he was doing it because he was thinking, or trying to keep from laughing. After all, Mike was city bred and born, and I'd recently learned he came from money. While he didn't make a mint on a detective's salary and he didn't live extravagantly, he made enough to live comfortably and stood to inherit a rather big fortune when his mother passed. I mused then that the closest he'd probably ever gotten to horses was the polo field, the race track, or to watch Olympic dressage events, which was akin to watching cement dry.

In another awkward moment I realized everyone was looking at me and I wasn't saying anything. "Uh, yeah."

"We have dogs and cats goin' missing all the time and we wondered what was happenin' to 'em. But then I found out this mornin'." Junior beckoned them to follow and started around to the back of the house.

Marge didn't follow, she just watched after us, staring me down until we rounded the side of the house and she could no longer see us. I was happy she didn't come along.

We crossed the backyard to a fenced-in area. Junior opened the gate and led us through it, closing it behind us. There were cattle in this enclosure. Most of them lingered near the water troughs and the lean-to shed a few hundred yards away. Junior kept walking and we followed. Enclosure led to enclosure until we were about a mile from the house. Directly ahead of us stood a barn.

"So, it's possible you just have coyotes?" I asked, knowing that oftentimes people would rather assign the guilt to Satanists or aliens rather than natural predators.

"Coyotes don't do nothing like this," he said, reaching the barn door and throwing the door open. "This barn is far away enough from the house that they can get in and out without being seen."

I was about to roll my eyes, but then my eyes fell on the make-shift altar at one end of the barn. Inch by inch I inspected the scene before me. Nope. It wasn't coyotes and it wasn't stupid teenagers dabbling. What Junior and Marge had were practicing Daemonolaters.

Though admittedly I was curious why they were doing their Ba'al Rites in Junior's barn. Of course there was nothing else in the barn… "What do you usually use this barn for?"

"Nothin' no more. I was using it for my ATVs, but we built the big shed up by the barn at the house. Now it's empty storage space." Junior narrowed his eyes. "I only came in here this morning 'cause I saw the door open a bit."

I stepped in ahead of Mike and Jerry and began surveying the coven's handiwork. I say coven because it had to be more than one Daemonolater as evidenced by the size of the circle of stones. Solitary practitioners often kept their ritual spaces smaller. Also, they'd swept the barn down and were keeping it clean. An abandoned barn this size should have been full of spiders and critters, but it wasn't. They weren't dabblers because dabblers didn't usually know the finer intricacies of blood magick, nor that working with Ba'alberith was more effective with the use of animal bones.

Sure enough, some animal bones sat on top of the altar. They did appear to be from small animals, like cats or dogs, but these bones didn't seem to have been macerated in a bone cleaning solution like one might expect from the bones of a sacrifice. No, these were *found* bones, probably procured in the desert after natural decomposition had taken place. Certainly they could send this stuff to a lab…

14

"So what do we have here?" Jerry asked. "Kids playing Satanist?"

I shook my head. "No, you have real daemon worshipers. But why here? Why risk trespassing for a Ba'alberith ritual?" I bent down and looked at a candle that was almost burned to the bottom. Something had been carved in it, but so much of the candle was gone I couldn't tell what. I looked at Junior, genuinely curious. "Do you have any enemies? Maybe someone who wants to see your farm go under?"

Junior just looked at me in horror. He was undoubtedly a God-fearing man.

Jerry stepped up. "You mean this is some kind of curse?"

I shrugged and pointed to the sigil of Ba'alberith painted on the barn wall above the altar. "Ba'alberith is a daemon of death. This is what remains of a blood rite."

"So they are killing animals then." Jerry shook his head. "I'm going to have to make a full report."

Mike finally stepped in. "Well we can't say they're killing animals. There aren't any bodies."

"We've got bones," Jerry pointed out.

"Yeah, but these appear to be bones that have been through the natural decomp process and that takes months. Even in the desert. Bones of a sacrifice would have to be prepared differently. They'd be cleaner, smoother, and whiter. These haven't been processed. It looks like someone found these bones," I said quickly. After all, if I'd really thought there was animal sacrifice involved, I would have said so.

I knew Mike would give me the benefit of the doubt. He did, and evidently I'd been with him long enough that his sick detective skills were starting to rub off on me. "Yeah, you could probably send the bones to the lab and they could tell you if they naturally decomposed or not."

"But, the blood," Junior protested.

"Probably pig or cow blood or even chicken blood. Is there a slaughter house anywhere nearby?" I asked.

Mike nodded in agreement.

"There ain't no slaughter houses near here. You'd have to drive a ways, but a lot of folks butcher their own meat," Junior said.

I narrowed my eyes and looked at Mike and he seemed to know exactly what I was thinking because he said it before I could. "So where would I go if I wanted to get some intestines and blood to make blood sausage?"

"Frank's Meat Market over in Sunnyvale," Jerry said, not seeming to get it.

That's where I stepped in. "It's the habit of some practitioners to get their blood from butchers or slaughterhouses under the guise of making blood sausage. You can get a lot of blood quickly and easily and you don't need to make an unnecessary sacrifice because the animals at a butcher or slaughterhouse have already been sacrificed."

"Lazy Satanists?" Jerry asked, seemingly amused.

"No, practical and efficient, and they may not be Satanists at all," I corrected, my voice a bit cool.

"But you said *devil worshipers...*"

"I said *daemon* worshipers. Some daemon worshipers are Satanists, some aren't."

Jerry gave Mike a strange look and Mike looked at me.

Was it really any wonder I was finding myself annoyed by Jerry? While Mike had been kind of a pain in the ass in the beginning, at least he had a few endearing qualities. Jerry, on the other hand, was just an idiot. Now I remembered why we never really dated. "So, you going to collect evidence for trespassing? Take pictures, have the bones and blood tested? Or do you want to leave and risk someone making all of this disappear tonight?"

"Liz has a point," Mike said.

"Yeah, yeah," Jerry said, obviously annoyed. "Let me go back to the car, call this in, get the camera and the evidence bags and stuff."

Junior nodded at Jerry. "You can drive on back so you don't hafta carry all that. I'll open the gates for ya."

Once Jerry and Junior were gone, Mike shook his head. "So what do you *really* think?"

"Someone who knows something about Ba'al rites."

"So this isn't just some kids messing around?"

"Looks like a bonafide Daemonolatry coven."

"Hmm."

"Well, on the upside the only thing they've done wrong is trespass," I reminded him. "And they've drawn the sigil of Ba'alphegor on this rock wrong. It's missing the cross mark there. They did it right on the wall though."

Mike nodded and bit his lip.

"Wait, you think something different?" I knew when he was biting that lip, he was thinking.

He pulled a lip balm from his pocket and put some on. "I think it's kids."

I frowned. "Why?"

"It's too by-the-book. Didn't you include a full Ba'al rite in the last book you wrote?"

My left eyebrow popped up and I looked back at the unmodified ritual space with only one sigil drawn wrong. If anything, a serious group would have made sure the sigils were drawn spot on, but they likely would have adjusted the ritual to reflect common practices of the coven. Most covens didn't do rituals without some kind of personal signature. "I see what you mean, but theoretically this is a Ba'alberith rite."

"Is it done properly and by-the-book or not?"

"Well, yeah," I had to agree.

"Too perfect and by-the-book shows inexperience, right?"

"Usually," I said, still not sure I agreed with him.

"Good. It's probably kids." He turned toward the door as Jerry and Junior pulled up in the patrol car.

I narrowed my eyes and said playfully, "Care to make a wager?"

"What are we wagering?" His eyebrows bounced playfully.

"Well nothing kinky while we're here," I said with a snicker. "My mother probably has hidden chastity cameras strategically placed around the house."

He chuckled, but his levity became suddenly serious. "On our way out of town we're stopping at the first hotel."

I laughed. "Okay, fair enough. However, I think this wager is on who has to drive the first leg back to Denver."

He shook his head. "Oh no. I'm not letting you drive. Also, you don't know how to wager. How about this -- if I'm right, and I think I am, you have to get a maid outfit and wear it for me at least once. If you're right, I will do one thing for you, even if it seems unreasonable or I hate it."

"This trip doesn't count."

He laughed. "No, this is my payback for making you deal with my mother. Family is never wagered because if I love you, I put up with your family and vice versa. That's a given."

Jerry and Junior finally got out of the car.

I started snapping pictures with my phone.

Mike bit his lip again and looked at Junior. "You and the wife have any kids?"

"Just Roy."

"How old is Roy?" Mike asked.

18

I smiled and shook my head. Junior and his wife didn't look like scholars, it was unlikely their spawn was either. Then again, I could have been wrong. Magick, to the extent this was done, had to be done by someone with a penchant for reading.

"Seventeen. Now you don't think Roy had anything to do with this...?" Junior's posture turned defensive. He adjusted his ball cap.

"I'm just saying kids experiment sometimes."

"He wouldn't kill animals," Junior started.

"There's no evidence here that any animals were killed." I reminded.

"But the blood," Junior said.

"It could be bought or obtained easily by kids raised on a farm." Mike gave him a broad grin. "Where is Roy right now?"

"At the gas station, working," Junior said.

"So no animal sacrifice and no trespassing?" Jerry clarified. A smug smile spread across his lips. "Then maybe you should see this."

The deputy whipped out his phone, pulled up some saved photographs, and turned the screen toward Mike. "We found this on the other side of town."

Sliding up alongside Mike, I peered at the screen.

"A coyote killed a rabbit?" I couldn't help myself because that's exactly what it looked like.

Jerry shook his head and swiped to the next picture. "We found the rabbit right outside of this."

It was my turn to bite my lip. Not because I was thinking on it, but because I wanted to laugh and biting my lip was the only thing that was going to help keep me from it. There, on the screen of Jerry's phone, was a pentagram made of stones. It could have been an inverse pentagram, depending on perspective, but the picture itself didn't look menacing and the corpse of the rabbit was about three feet away from it.

Mike seemed to be in step with my thinking. "Was the rabbit someone's pet?"

"No, but we're pretty sure it was a satanic sacrifice."

"You know," I said, wrapping my arm around Michael's waist. "I'm getting kind of hungry. I say we go have some dinner, we can discuss this, and maybe tomorrow we can go talk to Roy to see if maybe he has a friend playing a trick on him."

Junior nodded, "I'll send Roy down to talk to you at the diner if that's where you'll be. I didn't think it could be his friends."

"That would be great Junior. Let me take some pictures and a sample of some of the blood on these rocks, and the bones for the lab, and then we'll get out of your hair." With that, Jerry went about his job collecting *evidence*.

It was kind of disappointing that kids were behind it, but I should have known better. Now I owed Mike a night wearing a naughty maid costume. I frowned and started toward the car. "I'll be in the car. Wake me up when we get to the diner."

Mike followed, and climbed in the front seat. "So?"

"You get your night of naughty maid, what do you care?" I said with a laugh.

"I didn't say naughty. You added that part, but if that's what I'm getting, I'm into it." His grin extended from ear to ear.

Taming the beast, my boyfriend, for an entire week, was going to be a challenge. I wasn't even sure *I* could be celibate that long. Of course before Mike I'd gone a couple of years without.

Jerry joined us seconds later after having thrown the now filled evidence bags in the trunk. He started the car and

20

proceeded to turn it around. Then he slowly followed Junior as Junior opened each gate leading back up to the house and to the dirt road leading back into town. He waved at Junior and Marge as we left, then called in on the radio, and once we were assuredly on a highway in the middle of nowhere he said, "We've had other things happen like this in this town. I agree it's probably kids, but this stuff is dangerous."

In the rearview mirror, I caught Jerry's eyes on me when he said that last bit. "It's only dangerous if you don't know what you're doing or you use it foolishly."

"Do these kids know what they're doing?"

I shrugged.

Mike was wise enough to keep his opinion to himself.

"It's like they have an instruction manual. They have those, right? Books that tell people how to do it?" Jerry directed his question to me again.

"Of course. Just like any spiritual practice."

Turning to me Mike gave me a half-hearted smile. "You're tired."

"Aside from the yawning, how can you tell?" I closed my eyes, feeling Jerry watching me.

"Liz used to read about the occult when she was a teenager," he told Mike. "Everyone thought she was a witch."

"She certainly does love to read," Mike responded, cool as a cucumber.

I stifled a snicker.

Jerry dropped it when Mike asked them how their precinct handled organized crime. The conversation turned to immigration, drug lords, and illegal pot farms and I closed my eyes and let myself drift.

Max's hadn't changed one bit except they'd re-upholstered the booths. My stomach literally growled at how hungry I was, but first, I had to use the facilities. When I emerged from the restroom, I found Jerry and Mike had already found a booth and a tall, wiry, greasy brown-haired kid was sitting next to Mike. I was betting it was Roy.

I was right. Uncomfortable, I sat down next to Jerry, who moved over a little to give me extra room when he caught Mike looking at his proximity to me.

Roy turned from Mike and glanced at me. His eyes went wide with horror and he looked down at his hands.

"Guilty much?" Mike asked.

"No, really. I don't have any friends who do that sort of thing." His voice trembled.

Jerry noticed the young man's change in demeanor when I sat down at the table, too. Except he took it wrong because, well, Jerry didn't know I wrote books about Daemon Worship and that to that particular group of people, I was rather well-known.

It was obvious the kid recognized me. It was also obvious that we weren't going to get a straight answer out of the kid until we ditched Jerry.

"I can't really help you with anything else," Roy said.

"Oh, you might want to tell whoever did the sigils on the Ba'al stones that they screwed up Ba'alphegor," I told him as he got up to leave.

The teenager regarded me with sheer horror, but didn't say anything. He practically ran from the diner, glancing back from the parking lot.

"What does that mean?" Jerry asked, confused.

I shrugged. "I suppose it means he'll be calling his friends to let them know we're on to them."

Mike nodded, looking at me and the now empty spot next to him in the booth. I gratefully switched sides, leaving Jerry to himself and scooting in next to Mike, who immediately put his arm around me. Probably in some male display of dominance and ownership.

Ignoring the silent power-play I took up the menu and decided on the club sandwich for dinner.

Jerry kept his thoughts to himself while we ordered and when our food came. It was halfway through dinner when he finally said, "How come is it I feel like you two know something about my case that I don't?"

I shrugged. "I don't know. Why?"

"Nothing about Roy seemed strange to you?" Jerry leaned in, picking on me in particular.

"He was really nervous. I said what I said there to see if he'd freak out."

"Well he did." Jerry grabbed a fry off of his plate, dipped it in ranch dressing, and shoved it in his mouth.

"Yep," I agreed.

Mike skillfully changed the subject again and for the rest of dinner and on the drive home, he kept Jerry occupied with topics from bizarre cases to El Chupacabra.

Jerry dropped us off at eight-thirty, bidding Mike "Laters."

I shook my head as he drove off. "Did he really just say *laters?*"

"What's wrong with that?" Mike gave me an innocent look.

"Nothing I guess." I rolled my eyes and started up the steps, my key in hand. The parents weren't home yet.

Mike followed. "Yeah, I keep getting he doesn't like me very much."

"Who knows? He's probably jealous that I'm no longer single and on the market, though he didn't seem interested the last time I was here, or the time before that." Now, most women might have been flattered. Me, I wasn't so easily taken. "Don't worry, you have nothing to worry about. If I were interested in Jerry, I would have taken that chance years ago. There's not enough money or alcohol on the planet."

Mike laughed. "Oh really?"

"Yeah." We got into the house and closed the door behind us. I flipped a light switch that turned on several lamps in the living room.

"So maybe a *quickie* before your parents get home?" He laughed.

"Very funny. You think I'm kidding about chastity cams?" My eyes traveled the room, I honestly wouldn't have put it past her.

Mike looked taken aback. "It was worth a try. Bedtime then?"

"You tired?" I was.

"Yeah," he said, taking a seat on the couch. "I could definitely sleep."

"Me, too," I agreed. With that our first day in Sandpiper Point ended. Me in the spare room, him on the couch.

I don't remember my parents getting home, or the sun rising the next morning, or the smell of breakfast, or the sound of Jerry showing up. It wasn't until my mother came into the spare room and firmly shook me awake that I finally came to.

"What's wrong?"

"Jerry and Mike are going to do some detective work." Mom sounded really impressed. "Mike told me to tell you he'd be back later."

She stood and started toward the door. Her short brown hair was starting to turn a silvery gray. At sixty-five, it was bound to. I was surprised she wasn't dying it because my mother seemed to fight all the other signs of aging with Pilates and miracle skin creams.

"Oh good. It will give me an opportunity to go into town and grab some better toothpaste. I hate the stuff I brought."

"Well while you're out, could you stop and pick up my dry cleaning?" My mother called back on her way toward the kitchen.

"Yeah," I said. The toothpaste was an excuse, of course. I really wanted to get Roy alone at the gas station and find out what was going on.

The drive into town always took me back to my teenage years. Everything was the same save for a few buildings, some new fast food restaurants and a coffee shop. I stopped and picked up the dry cleaning first, then got myself a latte despite the fear that my *Starbucks* expectations would ruin the experience. Surprisingly, the latte wasn't bad and I made a mental note to bring Mike here before we left. I stopped at the gas station last.

Roy sat behind the counter at the cash register while a co-worker sat perched upon a stool a few feet away reading a car magazine. Roy didn't notice me at first. I grabbed a random tube of toothpaste and headed straight to the counter, plopping it down.

"Hi. Roy is it?" I smiled.

The young man's eyes went wide and his jaw dropped a little. "Yeah, um, will this be all?"

"This and I really want to know what's going on. This is my home town, after all." I put a ten down on the counter.

"Oh, you're from here?"

I nodded.

He rung up my toothpaste then asked, "You want a bag?"

"No, but I'll be in the parking lot finishing my latte if you find you want to talk." I gave him a kind smile and wandered out to the car.

I waited fifteen minutes, finished my latte, used my phone to check my email and social networking sites, and even checked my bank balance. He didn't come out. Finally, I pulled the car out of the parking space and up to one of the pumps. I figured I might as well fill the tank while I was here even though the car still had over quarter of a tank.

He came out while I stood there watching the digital numbers on the pump rapidly increase.

"My parents can't find out," he started.

"Well, I'm not in the habit of outing people. How long have you been practicing?" It was my experience the wrong question could easily make someone clam up, so I followed the question with a smile and, hopefully, relaxed body language.

"About six months. My girlfriend, Kelly, she and her aunt, one of the biology teachers at the high school, and a few others," he blurted. "I've read all of your books."

I kept smiling. Roy was definitely not someone you wanted keeping secrets for your coven. At least he'd broken his silence to the right person. This time. He wasn't a backwoods folksy kid either. Not by a longshot. He didn't have that twang in his speech that his parents did. Marge and Junior, not scholars themselves, had spawned a smart one.

I could see the relief on his face that he was able to tell me. "I figured since my mom and dad never used that barn it would be safe to use it for our Ba'alberith rite."

"What about the other incidents?" I said, then added, "Like the pentagram made from the stones?"

"We put four of them in the desert alongside roadways all around the town, for protection. We buried witch bottles under them," he said, obviously proud of himself for having helped.

"Well, Deputy Garza says they found a dead rabbit next to one, and he's decided the rabbit was a satanic sacrifice." I removed the gas nozzle from my tank, and put the cap back on, turning it until it clicked back into place.

"We don't do sacrifices."

"What about the blood for your Ba'al rocks?"

"Kelly's uncle raises and slaughters his own cows – for food. He just killed one a few weeks back," the young man said in earnest, then repeated, "We don't do animal sacrifice."

"I believe you, but the Sheriff's Deputy doesn't. Evidently he has more evidence and he knows there's a practicing group in this area. You guys haven't really done your part to keep things on the *down low.*"

"This is bad..." he said, getting nervous. "Her aunt could lose her job, some other people could lose theirs..."

"Well, the Deputy is going to figure it out. He's not an idiot. Either someone is going to have to come forward and sacrifice themselves for the good of the coven, or you can try to elude the police and this whole thing could be blown wildly out of proportion by superstitious, stupid people." That was the truth of it right there, and I didn't mind saying it. This coven needed to get their act together or they'd end up unemployable in Sandpiper Point and Pima County.

Roy took a deep breath.

"See if your girlfriend will step forward. Or will her parents flip out too?"

"I can't let her take the blame..."

"Who has the least to lose?" It was an honest question, and I knew from previous experience that when it meant saving the entire coven, it was a question that needed an answer, fast.

He didn't say anything, just looked at me as if he expected something more.

"Go back to your coven and find out which of you has the least to lose. One of you can save everyone else."

"It has to be me," he said. "Otherwise my dad will press charges for trespassing on whoever confesses."

I tried to hide a cringe and failed miserably. "How mad do you think your parents will be?"

"I'll probably be kicked out of the house, because the alternative is living without Kelly and going to church to appease them." The young man frowned.

"You can't tell Deputy Garza about the rest of the coven. You have to pretend you acted alone. Do you have someplace to go?"

"I can stay with Kelly and her aunt." The frown didn't move.

"Maybe Kelly can take the blame and you could convince your parents that you told her it was okay," I suggested.

"No, same thing. I'd have to dump my girlfriend *and* go back to church to convince them I wasn't influenced or taken by *the devil*." He seemed determined to play the martyr.

"I'm sorry, Roy, but it's the only way. After this, the coven needs to quit being so careless." I didn't mind pointing it out because it was the truth.

Roy nodded. "Thanks Ms. Tanner. I appreciate it."

"You're welcome." I smiled, and Roy turned and went back inside.

I drove home and spent the afternoon swimming in the pool. Jerry didn't drop Mike off until four.

Mike put on his swim trunks and joined me. When he was sure my mother was in the kitchen, immersed in the task of making more tea, he shook his head. "The meat market was a bust. No one has requested blood. Unless the person who got the blood works at the meat market. The local farms, same thing…"

"I already know what's going on." I gave him a knowing smile.

"Speculation or fact?"

"I went to the gas station to talk to Roy. I figured he'd be more forthcoming if it was just me. I was right." I had to shut up then because my mom returned with a fresh pitcher of tea and some glasses.

Mike gave me a desperate look then submerged himself beneath the water.

When he re-emerged my mom had gone back inside to grab towels.

"He admitted to being part of a coven, but get this – we're both wrong." I paused and looked toward the door. "There are, evidently, teenagers and adults in the coven. Which makes this whole thing kind of precarious. Because technically, they've done nothing wrong. It wasn't trespassing because it was Roy who invited them to use the barn for their Ba'alberith rites, and technically they haven't sacrificed any animals so there wasn't animal cruelty. If anything, they're guilty of practicing magick and ritual in a small town afraid of its own shadow."

"Hmm."

"This also means no maid costume." I couldn't hide the satisfaction in my voice.

"Oh damn." He laughed, then gave me a quizzical look. "Where'd they get the blood?"

"Roy's girlfriend's uncle has a small farm and just slaughtered a cow a few weeks back. I guess the plan is that one of the coven members is going to take the fall for the rest of the coven. Chances are it will be Roy." I shrugged, still not feeling right that a teenager was going to give up his parents in order to save adults who should have known better.

"So at worst, trespassing." Mike nodded. "But if Roy takes the blame, no charges."

"Yep."

Mike shook his head. "I thought people under eighteen weren't allowed?"

"Depends on the group," I said as my mom breezed out the back door with the towels.

We spent the rest of the afternoon and early evening in the pool while my dad barbequed.

Thursday morning, Jerry was back on my parents' doorstep looking anxious. Luckily my dad was at work and mom had an appointment to get her hair done so Mike and I were home alone.

"This is big and I don't know if I should go to the Sheriff with this yet," he started.

"Someone confess?" Mike asked, expecting, as I was, that that's what had happened.

"Yeah. Roy Gordon confessed, but it's bullshit. There's something bigger going on. It's not just Roy. I think the mayor of Sandpiper Point and half the city council is in this coven." Jerry paced the living room, full of nervous energy.

My jaw dropped.

Mike bit his lip, then said, "How do you figure?"

"Anonymous tip. I checked into a few things and whoever left the tip, it checked out. Roy is just the kid they threw under the bus to throw me off their trail."

Mike looked at me, as if I had answers.

I had nothing to offer, except maybe a bit of common sense. "Well, if we look at this rationally, we still can't prove there have been real animal sacrifices, and if Roy was in on it, you technically don't even have trespassing since presumably the coven had permission from Roy to use the barn. So at most what you have is a Satanic or Daemon Worshiping coven and nothing more. Last time I checked this was a free country and as long as it isn't hurting anyone or breaking any laws, people in this country have freedom of religion regardless what that religion is."

Jerry stopped in his tracks as if he'd just been slapped upside the head. "Well there has to be something illegal about it."

Shaking his head Mike said, "I'm pretty sure there isn't."

"We can't have a Satanist demon worshipping mayor and city council. This is a Christian town full of God-fearing citizens," Jerry started.

"Actually, that's not true if the mayor and half the city council aren't Christians. If your coven really is *that* big, then my guess is there are a significant number of other-than-Christians in this town and they have every right to be represented just like any other religious group," I corrected, my protectiveness toward my brothers and sisters in the arts showing.

"And you can't really say something they've done is illegal if you have no proof," Mike added.

"You both sound like you're defending them." Jerry's head whipped around to face me. "You know how dangerous talk like this can be…"

"What's your proof that the mayor is in this coven?" Mike asked.

"Someone told me to go to his house and look in the back window and I'd see a pentagram sun catcher in it, and if I went to the backyard, behind the fence, I'd find an outdoor temple with an altar and some of those same symbols. So I stopped by this morning, no one was home. I went out back and sure enough, I found the sun catcher, the temple, the symbols, all of it." He pulled out his phone and showed us the pictures.

My heart sank. Gods damn it. I spent the bulk of my free time helping high profile Daemonolaters who did their

31

best to stay *in the closet*. These folks, however, seemed determined to come out of that closet, pentagrams blazing. I couldn't change it despite my instinctive efforts to try to keep them under wraps.

"I have to tell the town. Warn people," Jerry said.

"No, don't do that!" There were a few times in my life I'd wanted to slap Jerry Garza, and this was one of those times.

"Why not? Don't you think your parents deserve to live in a town free from Satanists?" Jerry took a step toward me. "We can't allow this."

"Wait, just hear me out," I said, holding up my hands. "People are happy right now, right? Nothing bad is really happening. All you have is a slight mystery. A kid who confessed to using his parents' barn for a ritual. You can just let it go, drop it all, and not pursue any of this. Let people go on living their quiet lives."

Jerry looked at me dumbfounded. "But don't you…"

I cut him off. "Jerry, I'm a witch and I belong to a coven, and the people I practice with are good people."

Yeah, I was only telling a half truth. I was a Daemonolatress, but technically I was a witch, too. He didn't need to know the Daemon worshiping part. Chances are he'd think it was all the same anyway. I was right.

"You're in on this?" His jaw dropped.

"No, it's not like that. I didn't know what was going on until I talked to Roy yesterday at the gas station when I stopped for gas. He told me everything, well, except that the Mayor was a member. He just told me it was him, his girlfriend, her aunt, and some other people." I paused to see if he was hearing what I was saying because all the color had drained from his face. I told another lie. "I was going to tell you what Roy told me, today."

"So it really was true that you were a witch back then." His voice was quiet.

I nodded. "Afraid so."

He turned to Mike, "Did you know this?"

Mike nodded. "Yeah."

"You one, too?"

Again, Mike nodded. "Yes."

"What am I going to do?" Jerry asked absently to no one in particular.

"Nothing," I told him. "These people are the same people you've known for years. They're no different today than they were yesterday, except today you know they're not Christians. No crimes have been committed. They've just gotten comfortable and aren't hiding things as well as maybe they had been."

A knock on the front door stopped the entire conversation.

"Hello?" came a gruff voice from the front door.

"Sheriff?" Jerry asked.

"Deputy Garza?" The Sheriff, I don't recall his name, came through the front door cautiously. He was fifty-ish and graying, but he was still built. He almost looked like one of those rugged cowboys in an old movie. "Saw the car out front thought I'd check to make sure everything was okay."

"Uh, yeah, Liz Tanner is an old friend of mine, from school. This is the Denver detective I was telling you about. Michael Katz, this is Sheriff Riley." Jerry looked over his shoulder at me with a frown while Mike and the Sheriff shook hands.

I nodded politely at the Sheriff when he acknowledged me with a wide smile. That's when I saw it. There around the Sheriff's neck hung the seal of the Daemon Ba'al. I corrected myself silently. This wasn't just a Daemonolatry coven, it was a sect of Ba'al worshipers. They were Daemonolaters certainly, but Ba'al was their coven's patron Daemon.

Mike noticed it too, because when he caught sight of the pendant, a wide smile made its way across his lips.

Poor Jerry was working for a member of the very coven he wanted to expose and he was so clueless he didn't even know it.

"Well, what was the problem over at the Gordon farm?" he asked.

Jerry looked at me, then at Mike. There was a long pause. I could tell he had weighed the pros and cons and decided I was right. "Roy and some friends were playing a prank on some other friends, and they forgot to clean it up before Junior found it."

The Sheriff lifted an eyebrow and smiled. "Kids, huh? Well, come on and I'll buy you some coffee." Then the Sheriff turned to Mike and me, "You two want to join us? We have a nice little coffee shop in town."

I nodded. "Sure. I had a latte there yesterday. It was really good. Go ahead. We'll be along in a few."

The Sheriff nodded and smiled, then turned and left, followed by Jerry, who didn't look back even once. Once they were out of the house I went and grabbed my purse.

When I re-emerged from the bedroom Mike looked at me expectantly. "Well?"

"Well what?"

"Do you think he's going to tell?"

I let out a deep sigh and moved up alongside him. "I don't think so."

"Then why do you look so upset?" Mike put his hands on my waist and pulled me to him.

"Okay, I'm a little sad."

"Why?"

"How come there wasn't some huge Ba'al worshiping coven here when *I* lived here?"

Mike began laughing. "Elizabeth Tanner, you are something else."

He kissed my forehead, still laughing, and then released me and started toward the front door with car keys in hand.

I followed behind him skipping. "Then I could have told everyone I was from Sunny Satan Arizona…. Wait, no, Sunny Ba'al Arizona?"

The latter had a better ring to it.

Mike kept laughing, I kept skipping, and Sandpiper Point, Arizona went on as it always had, Daemon Worshipers baseball games, weddings and all.

FINIS

Dead Man's Knock

OTS # 3.5

(Read between Rising Darkness and Ascending Darkness)

To the Dead Man's knock!
Fly, bolt, and bar, and band!
Nor move, nor swerve,
Joint, muscle, or nerve,
At the spell of the Dead Man's hand!
Sleep, all who sleep! -- Wake, all who wake!
But be as the dead for the Dead Man's sake!

-- Thomas Ingoldsby, The Ingoldsby Legends

The severed hand in the window moved. I stopped dead in my tracks and looked at the storefront display. I'd never noticed this particular shop before, and I frequented this part of Colfax often. The one mile stretch was home to some of my favorite antique shops, used bookstores, and gourmet cafes. Mike, my boyfriend, kept walking.

"Babe, wait," I called to him.

He stopped and turned back toward me. "I thought we were going to Remy's for lunch."

"We are, in a minute. You have to see this." I pointed to the shop window, to the severed hand in the wooden box.

He wandered up next to me and peered in, immediately shaking his head. He knew what it was. "Oh no. You're not getting another one."

"What are the odds?" I felt a grin come over my lips, unbidden. This wasn't the first Hand of Glory I'd ever seen. I had one, affectionately named Jorge, almost identical to it sitting in our garage at home. As a practicing dark witch, even I knew how rare they were. I'd come upon mine by sheer accident while on vacation in California. I looked up at the shop's signage. *Mary's Treasure Trunk*, it said. The words *Antiques, Gifts,* and *Treasures* on the window gleamed at me in bronze colored paint.

"You're not getting another one," he repeated, matter-of-fact.

"Jorge needs a friend. Besides, this one could be a fake," I told him. I knew it wasn't, but I wasn't telling him that. Fake hands didn't move. Mike, a detective with the Cherry Hills Police Department, wasn't into the macabre like I was. He didn't mind my magic and demons or the fact that I'd turned our spare bedroom into a ritual chamber. After all, he came from a long line of traditional witches himself. What he didn't care for were the old-school tools like the human femur, the goat skull, and the Hand of Glory. He'd sequestered these ritual implements of mine to a storage room in the garage stating that they freaked him out. If it were up to me, our entire house would be filled with such things. I'd already gotten my way and began replacing all of his rustic Western art with images depicting everything from the Death Tarot, to a Qliphothic Tree of Death. Instead of our small house in the foothills resembling something from the old West it was starting to resemble a gothic horror novel.

I started toward the door. Mike followed with some reluctance. Behind the counter stood a short, plump woman who couldn't have been older than fifty. She seemed to be busy writing something down, but she paused long enough to acknowledge us. "Hello. Let me know if you have any questions."

"Thanks," I said, making a b-line directly toward the display window. "The Hand of Glory in the window...."

The woman frowned. "The what?"

"The hand in the box," I clarified.

"That creepy old thing? My boss's son brought that in here last week. What is it?"

She came out from behind the counter and joined us at the window, looking at the box.

"A Hand of Glory," I repeated. "It's the dried and pickled left hand of a hanged man. Hopefully a murderer if it was made properly."

She looked at me as if I had two heads.

Mike let out a nervous chuckle. The woman looked at him, then me. She seemed uncomfortable. Evidently my stoic pragmatism was making everyone nervous.

"Well, it can't be real..." She leaned in toward the hand as if she was going to pick up the box from the window, but seemed to think better of it. "Who would do that?"

"Witches." I gave her a quick smile.

Mike shook his head and stifled a groan.

The surprised look on the woman's face almost made me laugh.

"Why on earth..." She gave me a questioning look.

"It was thought that with a Hand of Glory, one could open all locks and, if one were a thief, one could enter houses at night and the Hand of Glory would keep all occupants asleep while the thieves went about their business. There are two types of Hands of Glory. Some only have one candle held by the hand like my one at home, or they're like this one where all five fingers have candles on them. The user of this particular hand would need to make sure the thumb stays lit, otherwise it means someone in the house is awake and the thieves could be caught." I loved the old folk-spells, regardless how gruesome, and my enthusiasm was all too apparent.

The woman gave me a strange smile and plucked the box from the window, lifting it up to view the sticker on the bottom of the box. "Well, he wrote not for sale on it."

She didn't sound apologetic at all and Mike seemed relieved.

It was my turn to frown. "Well that's too bad. Would you do me a favor and give your boss' son my card so if he changes his mind and wants to sell, he could give me a call? I'm kind of a collector as it were."

"Of course."

I left the card, gave her a kind smile and a goodbye and we left the small shop behind.

The day flew by in a torrent of shopping and eating, and ended with us sitting up in bed watching the pre-recorded season finale of our favorite show. I must have fallen asleep before it ended because when the bang, like a shovel falling on concrete, sounded somewhere outside, I sat straight up in bed in a dark room. Mike always turned the television off before he fell asleep. His body sat silent and still next to me. I stared at him for a moment noticing with relief that his chest rose and fell with each breath. For a cop, Mike was a sound sleeper, but not usually as sound as me. It was highly unusual for me to wake up to random nighttime noises. As a-matter-of-fact, friends always joked that I was likely to sleep through a herd of elephants running through the street.

Usually when I did wake up - there was good reason, and whatever tonight's reason was, it sent a cold chill up my spine.

The first two rules of horror films are never split up, never go to see what the noise is. If my life were a horror film, I would be dead already.

I slipped out of bed wearing sweats and a tank top, and put on my slippers, then tiptoed out of the bedroom and down the hall toward the living room. I stopped and held my breath when I saw the man's shadow pass the front window. He appeared to be holding a candelabrum, because there were four lights and each one flickered as he moved.

Every instinct, every nerve, every pore, told me something was horribly wrong. Yet instead of waking Mike I made my way through the shadows into the living room where I could see out onto the veranda and the garage beyond. There were two men. They were both dressed in all black. I gasped when I saw that one carried the hand of glory. A hand like the one I'd seen in the shop window earlier that day. The second man carried a flashlight in one hand and what appeared to be a pendulum in the other. The pendulum was leading them toward the garage, the garage where *my* hand sat in storage.

Knock, knock, knock.

I jumped and turned my head away from the window toward the knocking. It wasn't coming from the front door, or even the direction of the men, who were now at the garage door. No, the knocking came from the spare bedroom, our makeshift temple. I quickly decided that maybe I was hearing things. I shrugged it off - I had to wake up Mike.

Racing back into the bedroom I left the light off and I shook his arm, afraid turning on the light might make the robbers come back to the house. Mike didn't wake up. He gave a restless snort, but didn't wake up. I shook him again. It was no use.

"Mike!?" I said into his ear as loud as I dared. Nothing.

I groaned, realizing Mike was under the spell of the hand. But why wasn't I?

Knock, knock, knock.

That wasn't my imagination. I'd heard it. The *dead man's knock*. My eyes darted toward the sound. It was said if you heard knocking and it wasn't by human hands, it was a visitor from the other side. Usually they showed up as a warning or to give a message. If that was the case, their timing sucked.

Knowing presumably there was nothing I could do to wake Mike up. I took the cordless phone off the charger and dialed nine-one-one.

The phone clicked and died.

Knock, knock, knock.

It wasn't going to leave me alone until I took the message. I forced myself to concentrate on my attempt to call the police. My cell phone was dead. Mike's cell phone was locked and I didn't know his code to open it. I tried to wake him one more time with no success.

Knock, knock, knock.

Insistent spirit. I was more afraid of the men stealing Jorge than I was of the spirit in the spare bedroom. Since calling the police was no longer an option, my mind raced to possible spells I could use to counteract the Hand of Glory and the deep sleep Mike was beholden to. But why wasn't it working on me? *The thumb must not be lit, or it keeps going out*, I told myself. The lyrics to *Rage's Hand of Glory* ran through my mind in full metal:

"The hand makes successful robbery - well,

But just take care of the thumb
If it don't burn someone's not in the spell
And he'll discover your plan"

The tables were, hopefully, turned on my inexperienced robbers. I started down the hallway, wary of the door coming up on the left. I had to go in there.

Knock, knock, knock.

That infernal knocking again. "I hear you," I whispered.

I mustered up as much courage as I could because if I was going to get some mandrake root to do the spell to counteract the hand, I needed to get it from the room and that meant dealing with the spirit.

Throwing open the door I held my breath, my eyes widening when I saw it. The silver orb knocked up against the wooden box sitting on top of the altar. Knock, knock, knock. Then it darted into the ceiling and vanished. I looked at the box on the altar. It couldn't be...

I hurried to the box and opened it to find Jorge, my hand of glory, safely nestled inside, and I felt an evil smile make its way across my face.

Clearly the owner of the second hand would use his hand of glory for nefarious means, so why shouldn't I use mine to take his? By now they would be in the garage and he would be following the pendulum, no doubt being guided the same spirit of the dead, the silver orb, who'd moved Jorge into the house, out of the garage.

I picked up Jorge and a dried piece of mandrake root and then lit the candle in Jorge's hand. The hand sprung to life and gripped the candle for all it was worth. I pushed the piece of mandrake into the wax of the candle and whispered over it: "Make me invisible to my robbers that I may take from them what they sought to take from me."

I left Jorge, lit, on the altar. There was no way I was taking him with me just in case things went wrong. I didn't want him there for the men to find and take. Hopefully the pendulum would keep them guessing and not lead them back to the house.

Moving cautiously through the shadows, I slipped outside and made my way toward the garage. When I reached the door it stood open and the lights inside were on. I could hear the robbers rummaging through things.

"It's not here," one man said.

"It has to be in this locked room," the second said, probably watching his pendulum swing toward Jorge's last location.

They'd found my creepy magickal item storage room.

"Are you sure this is the right address?" the first man asked. I couldn't see them, but somehow I just knew he was the one holding the hand of glory, I was sure of it. My instincts were rarely wrong.

"This is what is says on her business card."

I slipped into the garage and behind some boxes in time to see the first man hand the business card to his friend. The second man set the hand of glory, which looked like some macabre candelabrum, on Mike's obsessively clean work bench. He examined the card, and set in next to the hand on the bench.

"Help me with this door," the first man said, grabbing a bolt cutter from Mike's tool wall. Both men wore all black and ski masks. As trite as it seemed, it did ensure that there was no way I could identify either one of them.

Sure enough, the thumb on the hand of glory wasn't lit. It looked as if the candle was almost gone on that finger.

There was a loud snap as the lock clanked to the floor, echoing through the garage. I heard them push back the latch on the door.

"Shit!" the second man whispered.

"Relax, the hand is lit, we're safe," the first man assured him as he turned the knob and went into *my room.* "The pendulum says it's in here."

They entered the room where I kept those things Mike refused to let me keep in the house. My eyes went to the chair next to the bench, then the extra locks Mike kept neatly on the bench in a red bowl. One was open so there would be no need for me to find a key to open a closed lock. It made things easier for sure. In that moment I was grateful to be with a man who was so obsessively neat.

Confident in the spell meant to render me invisible, I slipped up behind them, unseen, grabbed the open lock, slammed the door shut, relocked the latch, and shoved the chair under the door handle just in case the lock or the latch wouldn't hold the weight of two men. I took my business card off the bench and shoved it in my pocket, then grabbed the hand of glory and blew out the candles.

"I undo this spell. Awake," I whispered to the hand. The hand withdrew, wilting slightly as the magick left it.

I left the garage behind me and sprinted back to the house with the new hand. When I got inside, I locked the door, went to the spare bedroom, and blew out Jorge's candle.

"Mike?" I called.

This time he woke up immediately. "What? Liz? What's wrong?"

"Call the police," I told him. "Two guys broke into the garage and I've locked them in there."

Leaving the hands on the altar, neither one alight, I left the temple and shut the door behind me, hurrying to the living room window to watch the garage to see if either of them came out.

WITHIN DARKNESS | AUDREY BRICE

I could hear Mike up now, moving quickly to put his pants on. I heard him dial the phone. After giving the police the details, he came out of the bedroom into the living room to stand by my side. The garage door was now closed, but the light inside was on.

"What do you mean you locked them in there?"

"I ran out there, found them in my storage room, shut the door, relocked it, and put a chair under the handle," I said, as if it was something I did every day.

I could feel his eyes staring at me in disbelief. Two loud bangs came from the garage. "They're trying to get out."

When you're waiting for the police to arrive, mere minutes feel like hours, but they finally did come. The emergency lights from the police cars lit up the darkness, flashing against the side of the house and garage, and Mike ran out to greet them. Admittedly, I was surprised he hadn't pulled his own gun and gone out to deal with the robbers himself. Instead, he stood back and let the officers on duty deal with it.

I stayed in the house until both twenty-something men, now unmasked, were led from the garage in handcuffs. Mike came back into the house and shut and locked the door behind him.

"Aren't the police going to need more information?" I asked.

"I told them you heard the robbers, I went out and locked them in the storage room, and then I called the police." He bit his lower lip. "That's all they need to know."

"Oh," I said, realizing he knew there was more to the story and didn't want to complicate matters with magick.

"So, what really happened?" He read me like an open book.

I let out a resigned sigh and started toward our spare room temple. "Come with me."

Mike followed. I could feel his silent inward cringe.

When I opened the door and threw on the light, exposing both hands of glory sitting on the altar, his jaw dropped. I reached into my pocket and pulled out the business card, handing it to him.

"Evidently the shop owner's son makes house calls. You were under the hand's spell. That's why I couldn't wake you up when I heard them. The thumb didn't light, which is why I didn't fall under the spell. I used Jorge to steal their hand, and lock them up," I concluded.

"How did you get Jorge out of the garage? Has he been in here all this time?" Mike's brow furrowed with worry.

"I'm not exactly sure how Jorge got into the house. I thought you brought him in as a joke," I lied. I knew, sort of, how he got into the house. It was the dead man's knock, but I wasn't telling Mike that.

Like usual, he knew there was more to the story, but he didn't ask. Instead, he shook his head. "Tomorrow I am fixing the garage door and the storage room door, and tomorrow, *both* of *those* are going back in there."

"But what if someone else tries to steal them? They're obviously dangerous in the wrong hands," I countered. No, if someone was going to try to steal the hands of glory, I wanted them to break into the house, where Mike or I could shoot them.

Mike groaned. "Babe..."

He paused for a long moment as if rethinking and then shook his head. He knew they were safer here than anyplace else. As a police officer he had to know it was for the best that they were in our possession and not someone else's.

Turning around, he left the spare room and started toward the bedroom. I followed, clicking off the light and shutting the temple door behind me. "Well?"

Kicking off his shoes he sat down on the edge of the bed. "What are we calling this one? Floyd? Abner perhaps?"

I gave him a half-hearted laugh and took off my slippers. "Abner has a nice ring to it."

"Jorge and Abner," he said, shaking his head. Then he clicked off the light.

That night my dreams were filled with the dead man's knock, bringing with it the knowledge that the spirits were with me, and all was right with the world.

FINIS

Rocky Mountain Haunt
OTS # 4.4
(Read between Ascending Darkness and Illuminated Darkness)

"Elizabeth? Do you have the ring?" he asked from the hallway in a hollow voice.

Normally this wouldn't have sent me jumping out of bed and straight out of my skin, except for the fact that I wasn't expecting anyone and I'd locked up before coming to bed. Not to mention I was the only one in the house. Mike was working late on a task force car theft case. My skin prickled and a cold shiver went up the back of my neck. I got up and started toward the bedroom door. Maybe I was hearing things.

"Hello?" I called into the dark hallway. I grabbed the broom leaning against the dresser and cautiously poked my head out of the bedroom door. When no response came, I took a few steps into the hallway. "Hello?"

Whoever it was obviously knew my name. Still, no answer. The house was big, much bigger than my old house that had to be rebuilt after a tornado, and certainly bigger than Mike's. We'd kept those houses as rentals when we bought this place. I made my way down the hallway, turning on lights and looking into every box-filled room. We were still fixing the place up.

Ideally, I wanted to wait to move in until the renovations were done, but we didn't want to pay two mortgages, so it made more sense to rent Mike's old place and move into the new house right away. My old house had been rented to a young couple months ago.

"Hello?" I called again. Maybe it was just a dream. It wouldn't be the first time I'd woken up from a dream thinking it was real.

No one was there. Then, downstairs on the first floor, I heard heavy footsteps in the kitchen. Now that – that wasn't a dream. I pinched myself to make sure I was awake. I was. That feeling of not being alone overwhelmed me and I slipped down the stairs as quiet as I could muster, toward the kitchen with my broom clenched in my hands, hoping I didn't just bring a broom to a gun fight. I had a gun, but I was still uncomfortable with it, even after a few sessions at the firing range with Mike. I heard a cupboard open, then close. I tiptoed through the hall and into the kitchen. Wasn't this how the victim always ended up dead in horror movies? *You never go investigate the noise*, my mind screamed.

Flicking on the light I fully expected to see someone standing there, but there was nothing. I breathed a sigh of relief, perhaps too quickly because the basement door off the mud room slammed shut, and the footsteps stomped down the stairs. Another cold chill ran through me and I dropped the broom with a loud clatter on the yellow linoleum floor.

I cringed and looked toward the door. The footsteps halted abruptly. I had two choices. I could follow whoever was in the house into the basement, or I could get the hell out of the house and call the police. I'm not a coward by any means, but I'm not stupid either. Even though I stood clad in pajamas and stocking feet, I turned tail down the hall, grabbing my purse, car keys and cell phone before getting the hell out of there.

Safe in the car parked on the street with all the doors locked, I called 911. Then I called Mike and left a voicemail. It took a policeman all of five minutes to arrive, and only a few seconds for his patrol car, even though silent and without lights blaring, to wake up the entire neighborhood. Well, okay, I'm exaggerating. Only the neighbor and the house across the street had lights go on. I got out of the car and waved at the officer.

He got out of his patrol car and came to stand next to me. We both looked up at the house.

"I have an intruder in my basement. Or I think that's where he was," I told him.

"Is there another way out?" he asked. We were both strangely calm.

"Yes. Through the back door." I said, my eyes darting to the skeletal frame of the house. For some reason, standing out here it didn't look like our house. Against the night sky it appeared menacing. Its features, every window and door frame, dark and foreboding. Had I seen the house at night first, I definitely would have had second thoughts. It really did look haunted right then. That's when I realized all the lights were out. When did that happen? "I didn't leave all the lights off. I left the upstairs bedroom light on, the hallway, the kitchen…"

Another patrol car showed up and another officer got out. The first officer lifted an eyebrow. "The power might have been cut!" he called to the second officer.

A sinking feeling gripped my stomach, but I brushed it away. I refused to give in to fear. The house appeared to be in a relatively safe neighborhood. That was one of the things Mike insisted on before we even started looking.

As the three of us stood there and looked up at the house, we all saw the dark shadow pass the uncovered window in the living room. Even with the lights out, there was still enough contrast to make the figure out.

"He's in there," one of the officers said. The second called it in, then said to me over his shoulder, "You stay here."

With flashlights drawn, both men hurried to the house and went inside. I stood on the street, helpless to assist them, watching flashlights bounce through the drapeless windows of our old Victorian house.

A dark-haired woman, no more than twenty, wearing a long, white nightgown joined me on the street. "You live here now?

"Yes," I said, thinking it was an odd question. The fact that she was wearing a nightgown in the middle of a cool autumn night, outside, was a bit odd, too. One might have put on a robe at least. I rubbed my arms, realizing I should have worn a robe, too. Or grabbed my hoodie.

"They won't find him. He's good at hiding. That one definitely has to go," the woman said.

The hair on my arms stood straight up and I turned to look at her, but I was alone on the empty street and the dark haired woman in the long white nightgown had vanished, if she ever existed at all.

After a few minutes, the officers started through the house turning on lights, one-by-one. I watched them move from room to room until all the lights from the basement to the main floor were on. Then they moved to the second floor, and finally the attic. We didn't have window coverings on any of the windows except the bedroom. Mike tacked up a temporary sheet so no one could look in. The window coverings were supposed to come in tomorrow morning and

Mike promised me that he and some guys from work would get them installed by early evening since it was Saturday.

Finally, one of the officers opened the front door and beckoned me back into the house.

When I got inside, I noticed they both looked a little nervous.

"Do you have someplace you can stay tonight?" the first one asked, a bead of sweat on his forehead.

I gave them an inquisitive look. "Why? He got away, didn't he? Do you think he'll come back?"

"See, that's the problem, Ma'am. We saw someone in here. When we got in here, we heard him in the kitchen, then we heard him running down the stairs into the basement. We followed. No one is down there, and all your doors and windows are locked except this front door here. None of the windows are broken. We've searched every room, closet and cupboard. So either you have a secret room in your basement that someone is hiding in, or you have ghosts. Either way, I don't recommend you stay here tonight," said the second officer.

Any normal person might have ran screaming from the house then and there, but I balked. A hidden basement room? That suggestion freaked me out far more than the idea of ghosts. Ghosts I knew how to handle. Judging from my mysterious encounter with a specter out on the street, I guessed ghosts were far more likely than a hidden room in the basement.

"My fiancé is a detective with the Cherry Hills police. I'll call him to let him know what's going on, and I'll just have a friend come stay with me for tonight."

Both men looked at me like I had two heads.

"If I was you, Ma'am, I'd go stay with the friend, just to be safe," the second said.

"You guys just buy this place?" the first asked.

I nodded. "Yeah. Moved in two days ago."

He shook his head. "I have to agree with Officer Franklin here. I wouldn't stay here. Maybe we should stick around while you pack a bag and we'll help you turn off all the lights and make sure it's locked up tight before you go."

The second, Officer Franklin, nodded. "We can't, in good conscience, let you stay here."

Upstairs a door slammed, and the footsteps started in the kitchen again.

"Maybe we should just leave the lights and get out," the first suggested. I could tell by the way they herded me out the door that if they could have run from the house without sacrificing their manhood, they would have. I paused to lock the front door from the outside, not sure I wanted to leave the house with all the lights on. The officers refused to let me linger any longer than necessary and urged me down the steps to my car. I paused at the sidewalk and looked back at the lit up house. The officers did the same.

As if the ghost knew what I was thinking, one by one the lights in the house began to turn off.

"Son-of-a-bitch. Lady, you should either get a priest in here or sell it," the first said, sheer horror in his eyes. "This is the creepiest thing I've ever seen."

Officer Franklin just shook his head. He looked a little pale.

Together, the policemen went back to their patrol cars, watching to make sure I got into my car. I did, and immediately called my best friend Alyssa.

Her boyfriend Gabe answered. "Someone better be dead."

"They are, and they're squatting in my house."

"What?" came the confused voice on the other end of the phone.

"My new house has an annoying ghost. It scared the shit out of me. Can I come sleep on your couch? Just for tonight."

"Liz?" Gabe's voice sounded more alert now and I could hear Alyssa stir in the background. Then I heard him say to her, "It's Liz. She's got a ghost and wants to stay here."

"What? Give me the phone." I heard her grab it from him. "Liz? What's going on?"

"I have a freaky ass ghost and I'm going to stay with you guys tonight. Just for tonight. I'll figure out how to deal with it tomorrow. I'm so tired," I said as the first police car pulled away. Putting my key into the ignition, I started my own car and put my seatbelt on.

"What happened?" Alyssa pressed. "Didn't you smudge the house and ward all the doors and windows *before* you moved in?"

"I'll be there in ten minutes." It was one in the morning and traffic was bound to be non-existent.

"Okay." Alyssa sounded disappointed that I was going to make her wait a whole ten minutes to hear the story, but she'd have to wait. "See you in a few minutes."

"Bye." I ended the call before she could say anything else, then carefully pulled away from the curb, leaving my dream house and all her ghosts safely behind me.

***

"Of course I did the smudging ritual and anointed all the doors leading outside and the windows. With protection oil – my own blend. Except maybe I didn't do the basement…" I cringed. Yeah, I'd been a bit lax.

Alyssa gasped and then scolded me as if she were my mother, "So you basically did a half-assed job."

I groaned. "Maybe a little half-assed, but chances are my half-ass protection is what woke up the ghost to begin with."

Gabe nodded. "Could be."

"What did it say to you again?" She scrunched her face as if the expression itself would bring her answers.

"It said, *Elizabeth, do you have the ring?*" I gave her a shrug.

"So wait – it wanted a ring?" Alyssa narrowed her eyes and wrote the word *ring* on the pad of paper next to her, and then underlined it three times. "I mean, at least it didn't try to hurt you."

"No, but it seemed to keep trying to lure me, and the police, into the basement." I shuddered. That was the one place in the house that did make me feel a little uneasy, but basements did that to everyone, or so I'd heard. That's why the creepy basement feeling wasn't a deal-breaker when we decided to buy.

Gabe sat back and listened, scratching at the horrific beard he wore. I was surprised Alyssa hadn't made him shave it off. It looked an unruly mess.

"Maybe the ring is in the basement." She wrote the word *basement* on her pad of paper and thoughtfully chewed the end of her Bic pen.

Gabe lifted an eyebrow and yawned. Clearly he was unimpressed with my haunting tale. "Tomorrow we'll check the basement for a ring. In the meantime, I'm going back to bed."

Alyssa shook her head. "Tomorrow, you're calling your crew, and you're going to do a ghost hunt while Liz, Mike, and I work on the house."

"That works, too," Gabe said, heading back to the bedroom.

I yawned then. "I think he has the right idea. Sleep now, ghosts tomorrow."

With a pout, she relented. "Okay, fine, but my alarm goes off no later than eight and we discuss it in the morning."

"Very good." I paused long enough to send Mike a text letting him know I was staying with Alyssa for the night due to ghosts, then I settled in on the couch along with Alyssa's gray tomcat, Felix.

***

I awoke to Alyssa shaking my shoulder and waving a phone in my face. "It's Mike."

Gabe walked into the living room putting on a shirt. "How long on that coffee, Liss?"

"I haven't started it yet," she groaned.

"Hey," I said into the phone.

"You guys want to meet me at BL's Diner for breakfast?" His voice sounded weary from a long night.

"Yeah, are you home?" I put my hand over the phone, "Forget the coffee Liss, we're going to BL's for breakfast."

Gabe immediately perked up.

Mike yawned into the phone. "No, still here. I'm reading your texts though and it sounds like you had an eventful night."

"You think?" I deadpanned. I hated it when he worked nights. It usually only happened occasionally when he was assigned to late night ops for some task force or another.

"We'll talk about it over breakfast." He knew me well enough to know I wasn't going to go into it over the phone. I hated talking on the phone.

"Yeah," I agreed. "We might be there early so we'll get a booth. Gabe needs his coffee or he's going to flip out."

Mike laughed. "Okay. See you in a few."

After I hung up I sat up on the couch and looked down at myself. I was still in my pajamas – a pair of pink pants with stars all over them, and a light gray tank top. I didn't even have shoes on. Just a pair of dingy gray socks.

With a chuckle, Gabe called over his shoulder, "Grab Liz some clothes and shoes while you're in there."

"Okay," Alyssa hollered back.

A few minutes later she emerged from the bedroom with a pair of black yoga pants, a pink t-shirt with flowers on it, and a pair of slip on flats. I knew we wore the same shoe size, but Alyssa was at least four inches taller than me.

I took the clothes from her and retreated to the bathroom to put them on. While the t-shirt was a bit large, the pants hit me right at the ankle. They must have been mid-calf length on her. Either way, at least I now looked somewhat dressed. So far it had been warm for October, so warmth wouldn't be a concern.

When I returned to the living room, they were ready to go, and without fanfare we left Alyssa's townhome behind us, got in our separate cars, and made our way to BL's.

It took almost thirty minutes for Mike to get there. Gabe was already on his second cup of coffee while Alyssa and I were finishing up our first.

Mike looked like crap. The last thing he needed was me banging around the house working while he was sleeping, but really I'd only planned to unpack boxes most of the day. I'd already cleaned the kitchen, dining room, and living room before the movers brought everything in, and I'd moved the area rugs and furniture where I wanted it. The exception were the bookcases. We had a study opposite the living room, but I wanted to take down the old peeling wallpaper and give it a fresh coat of paint first. On the main floor, beyond some closet shelves that needed to be put in, and some bathroom renovations, the unpacking was all that was left. The second floor was another story. We had four bedrooms now, one of which would be turned into a permanent temple, one a dedicated guest room, and one would become our office, but all of those rooms needed more work. Right now we were staying on a mattress on the floor in the room that would become our office because the master bedroom had to be renovated before we could actually move in. Both upstairs bathrooms needed paint and flooring and one of them needed a new sink and tub. At least the toilets and the master shower worked. Our bedroom set currently sat in the detached garage, along with our dressers and night stands. My biggest worry was the house would look barren since we had more space now, and no furniture to fill it. Alyssa promised to help me pick up the curtain rods and blinds, and unpack, while Gabe agreed to hook up our entertainment center. Now, he also planned to set up his ghost hunting equipment.

I waited until Mike had some coffee and everyone ordered before I told him the story about the night before. When I'd finished, I sat back and waited for his response.

"Why does this not surprise me?" He yawned and ran one hand through his dark hair.

I knew what that meant. Leave it to us to pick the most haunted house we could find – by accident.

Alyssa shook her head. "Nah, it's probably just a pissed off spirit tethered here by unfinished business. I can get rid of it."

Mike lifted an eyebrow. Alyssa had yet to prove her talents as a necromancer to him. Ever since the incident at Kylie Ramone's, where the spirit of a dead satanic priest possessed a woman who, in turn, stabbed me, he'd been skeptical.

"Why don't we just have Liz get Jorge out of the garage and do what she did to get rid of Leon?" Mike didn't elaborate because the waitress showed up with our breakfast.

Alyssa waited until she was gone. "That was a murderous spirit who was trying to get back to the land of the living. This one is just looking for a ring."

She sounded so sure of herself.

"So you don't think it's harmful?"

She shook her head. "It sounds like maybe it's just going to be annoying and loud until it gets its ring."

"Well, it's creepy because it knows my name," I said, putting another forkful of egg into my mouth.

"Spirits can easily get that information," Alyssa said as if it was no big thing. "We just have to find a way to keep him quiet so you can sleep and not think you have intruders."

"Amen to that," Mike said with half closed eyes. "Because I could really use some sleep."

We spent the rest of breakfast hatching the plan to catch a ghost. When we were done, Mike went home, and Alyssa, Gabe, and me swung by the home store to pick up curtain rods and the blinds I ordered. Then we went back to the house. Everything outside looked normal and the house had taken back its charming curb appeal that made me fall in love with it to begin with. It was your typical autumn day and I imagined again how fantastic the outside was going to look when I decorated for Halloween, making a mental note that it was only a few weeks away. When we got inside, Mike was already upstairs, and from the sound of his snoring, fast asleep. Our ghost hadn't impressed him, or scared him. I tiptoed upstairs to check on him and then came back down to find the house calm.

Alyssa was in the kitchen unloading a box of dishes and Gabe went from his car to the foyer bringing in his ghost hunting equipment. The house seemed perfectly quiet and normal. Not a footstep or disembodied voice to be heard, nor specter to be seen.

"So I'm going to set up in the basement, first," Gabe said, setting a case on the kitchen island.

"You want us to go with you?" Alyssa asked. "It would be a good opportunity to look around for a ring."

She looked excited to go. This wasn't the first time she and Gabe had seen the house. They'd helped us move, but this was the first time they'd been to the basement.

Gabe shrugged and picked up the case again. "Yeah, sure."

I followed with a sigh and we went to the basement. Everything remained quiet. Our basement is really nothing out of the ordinary. Creepy, yes. Most unfinished basements are. They usually smell like earth, they harbor spiders, and you can't help but feel something sinister lurks just beyond the light in the dark shadows behind the stairs.

With a shudder, I examined the bare concrete floor. While some creepy basements had walls or partitions, others mazes of bizarre rooms, this one was mostly open. Mike was actually considering finishing it and turning it into his man-cave. It was a good size for it. Over twenty-five-hundred square feet. We really had gotten a great deal on this place, but then now I knew why. Chances are the ghosts had scared off previous owners.

"This is cool," Gabe said, getting to work and setting up his cameras. He probably saw its potential as a man-cave, too.

"Okay, help me search for a ring," Alyssa said, drawing my attention from Gabe's temporary camera installation.

We walked around the entire basement, looking into every corner. Alyssa searched for secret compartments and even went under the stairs. The walls and floors were solid. No hidden rooms or secret passages. It was just a plain, old basement.

WITHIN DARKNESS | AUDREY BRICE

"If there was anything here, it's long gone now," I said. *Great*, I thought. *If the ghost wants a ring, and I can't give him the ring, then maybe I can't get rid of him.* I frowned at that thought.

As if she read my mind Alyssa said, "Don't worry, ring or not, we'll make sure our ring-guy either sees the light, or we send him off by force. I know a guy, a bouncer named Bune."

I let out a nervous laugh. Calling in the Daemon Bune was like calling in Special Forces to deal with a schoolyard bully, but then I know why Alyssa suggested it. Last time we encountered a spirit that refused to go voluntarily, she had been reluctant to call in the big guns, and I ended up with a knife in my gut. I never blamed her for what happened, but I think she kind of blamed herself. This time, she wasn't going to let it escalate. Instead, she was willing to bring in a Daemon to take a human spirit out. I could respect that.

With nothing to go on and with Gabe finished installing his cameras, we all retreated back upstairs to the warmth of the rest of the house. Gabe continued setting up and Alyssa and I had the entire kitchen unpacked and looking lived in by the time Mike made his way downstairs in search of food. I hadn't gone grocery shopping, though we had soda and water in the fridge.

"The guys should be here in a bit to help put up the drapes and blinds," he started, wandering over to Gabe's monitors on the dining room table. "Damn, you've been busy."

Gabe nodded. "Every room except your current bedroom is covered. I was waiting until you got up. I also managed to hook up your cable down here."

"I appreciate that." Then he turned to me. "What's for dinner?"

61

"I ordered some pizza. I'll go grocery shopping tomorrow." I looked around the kitchen and dining room, pleased that all the now empty boxes were in the mudroom off the back laundry room. I still couldn't believe this house was ours.

"Good. I'm over the fast-food diet." He ran his hands through his dark hair. The doorbell rang. He went to answer it.

"Jesus Christ man, you had to move into this scary fucking mansion? How much are they paying you?" It was his old partner, Smith. A couple of other guys, one I recognized as Sergeant Kale, stepped into the foyer, looking around. Kale carried a case of light beer.

"We got a good deal on it," he told them. "Besides, Liz has a good job and you guys know I'm living off of her."

They all laughed and Gabe shook his head. Alyssa snorted. I shook my head, too. That was the running joke now that I was making six figures working for the network. It sure beat the job at the print shop and being the clean-up lackey for the OTS, even though I was still a card carrying member. I did make more than Mike though, and even Mike's mom was happy about that. Beverly could now tell all her friends that her soon-to-be daughter-in-law was an executive for a cable network. While I may have come up in the world, my relationships with the dead and the Daemonic were the same as they'd always been. Bizarre, unsettling, and sometimes downright dangerous.

Smith noticed the array of monitors on the dining room table. "What's this? You putting in a major security system?"

"We're just checking for ghosts," Gabe told him.

With a laugh, Smith thought he was joking, then stopped when he realized Gabe was serious. "You're not kidding."

Mike shook his head. He caught a lot of shit at his own precinct for hooking up with me after the Chloe Brigid case. They called me *the witch*, which bothered Mike far more than it bothered me. He would undoubtedly catch a lot of shit for hosting a ghost hunt at the house, too.

He let out a sigh and said, "Liz called the police last night because she thought someone broke in. So they come check out the house, and they saw and heard the same things she did. Problem is, there was no one in or out of this house, but they all saw the figure of a man going through the rooms, heard the footsteps…"

"You're fucking with me." Smith wore a look of sheer disbelief.

"Hmm," said Kale. He was another non-believer.

Mike shrugged and tried to sound nonchalant. "They say they saw something. If it was just Liz I would have chalked it up to too many horror films and a bad dream. But it wasn't just her. So if Liz wants Gabe and his ghost-hunting pals to check it out, that's what we're doing. We'll see if they get anything."

"Well I've got to see this," Smith said. "Can we stay and watch?"

"You can stay and even help if you want," Gabe said. His ghost hunting team consisted of him and three other guys. Undoubtedly the extra man-power would help him gather evidence more quickly, which was good. I didn't want to be up all night long.

"Fine, but if they find something, don't run out of the house screaming like a sissy," Mike told him with a half grin.

Kale and the guy with him laughed.

"Well let's get these damn drapes up, huh?" Smith said, ignoring Mike's jab.

Gabe went upstairs to set up the last camera, and Mike and the guys began putting up drapes while Alyssa and I directed them. The pizza arrived an hour later. Two hours after that, Gabe's crew showed up. One hour after that – I had a house with proper window coverings and eight men discussing hunting ghosts while Alyssa and I looked on.

We might have missed the sound of footsteps coming from the kitchen had there not been a lull in the conversation.

"What the fuck?" Mike said, starting toward the sound.

"Right there," said one of Gabe's friends, pointing at the monitor.

We all huddled in a tight group around the monitors, watching in disbelief. No matter how many times you saw it, you always wondered if you were seeing things. When the house went silent and the footsteps stopped tromping down the stairs, Gabe rewound the video and we watched it from beginning to end.

The video clearly showed a semi-opaque shadow walking through the kitchen, even with the lights on. Then something even more disturbing happened. Another shadow ran behind it and it sounded like a door opened. The camera pointed at the stairs leading to the basement showed the door open, and then the cameras in the basement caught the two forms coming down the stairs and confronting one another at the bottom. Then both forms vanished.

I took a deep breath. Something violent had happened in this house and its ghostly residents appeared doomed to re-enact it night after night.

"Okay, you guys are fucking with us." Smith wasn't convinced.

I finally spoke up. Smith and his wife had always been kind to me, so I was gentle. "Unfortunately, no. I think Mike and I just bought an *authentic* haunted house. Not on purpose, mind you."

"Now we just have to figure out how to either get the spirit to leave on its own, or remove it forcibly," Alyssa said with a bright, perky smile.

"That's fine, but we'd like to get more evidence. Try to communicate with them if we can," Gabe said. Then to Alyssa, "Before you get all gung-ho ghostbuster on its ass."

The guys all laughed, leaving Alyssa exasperated as evidenced by the annoyed sigh and frigid glare she gave Gabe.

After calling the living room, I grabbed a recorder and went and sat on the couch by myself while the guys broke off into teams and split up, each taking their own part of the house.

Alyssa came up behind me, quiet like, and just stood there.

I didn't turn to her. Instead, I pressed the record button and said in a rather sarcastic tone, "Calling all ghosts in my house. What's up?"

"The ring lays beneath."

I shrugged. "It might, but I'm not digging up the cement floor down there to find it."

That's when I realized it wasn't Alyssa who was standing behind me. The voice was much softer and not nearly perky enough.

"You can make it rise."

Then I felt the hand on my shoulder and I jumped with a yelp and turned to face my ghostly companion. I was alone and my yelp summoned Gabe from the dining room. "What happened?"

"I just had another ghost conversation with nightgown girl." Then I realized I had the recorder in my hand. I turned it off and took a deep breath. "I was just startled, that's all."

"You got it on the recorder?"

"I hope so." I held the small box out to him and he took it.

I almost didn't want to hear it.

Gabe rewound and hit play. We listened to the conversation play back. It sounded just like I was having a conversation with an old friend. Her voice sounded the same on the recorder as I'd heard it.

"I think she's the one we need to talk to find out about our ring ghost. She doesn't have a high opinion of him," I told Gabe, trying to lighten the heaviness I felt.

He nodded. "Okay, once everyone gets back, maybe we can do a communication session in this room."

"She might be shy. She only seems to show up when I'm alone," I said.

"Will you be okay alone with her then?" Gabe looked around as if he expected to see her materialize. "If so I won't alert the others and I'll go back to the dining room."

I shrugged, feeling a bit unsure of myself. "Yeah, I think it will be fine."

Gabe checked to make sure the recorder was ready to go so I wouldn't erase the evidence already there, then he handed the device back to me. Once he was sure I was okay, he disappeared back into the dining room.

With a deep breath, I sat back down on the couch and hit record. "If there's anyone here..."

Of course there's someone here, I scolded myself. Then I felt her behind me again.

"How many of you are there?" I asked. I wasn't accustomed to living in a house inhabited by spirits.

"Four, including Daniel."

"Is Daniel the one looking for a ring?"

Pressing the ghost didn't seem to make her answer any faster. She took her time as if she had all the time in the world for a conversation.

"Of course. I don't think he means it as you do."

That was an odd turn of phrase. I found myself frowning. "Why?"

"The ring of power lays beneath," she said. Then she stepped through the couch and I felt her cold presence to my right.

I forced myself not to look directly at her because I knew she'd vanish if I did. But I could see her out of the corner of my eye and she looked as solid as any human. "Do you mean like a circle? Like a magick circle?"

"Katherine!" bellowed a voice from above. A cold blast of air hit me in the face, knocking me back, and just as quickly I felt chilled to the bone. My teeth literally chattered.

Gabe raced back into the living room, wild-eyed. "Did you see that?"

I shook my head and got up, clicking off the recorder. "No, but I felt it. I need my coat."

He disappeared back into the dining room, excited about something. Perhaps cold blasts of air or whatever he caught on camera. Whatever it was, I wasn't sure I wanted to see it just yet.

It was only a few steps into the foyer to grab my hoodie, but I thought better of it when I saw the dark figure standing near the door in the corner next to the coat rack.

"Shit," I whispered under my breath.

"He won't leave," the dark form said in a low, masculine voice before vanishing.

Gathering up my nerve was easy enough, especially with how cold the house suddenly seemed. I grabbed my coat off the coat hook and started back into the living room just as Mike and Smith came down the stairs.

"This ghost hunt is boring as shit. Got anymore beer?" Smith asked. Clearly sitting around in the dark, waiting for something to happen, wasn't Smith's cup of tea.

"Yeah," Mike said, equally bored. He noticed I had my coat on. "It is kind of cold in here."

"You should step into the living room," I told him. "It's really cold in there."

"Maybe after another beer," Mike said with a laugh.

Of course I really didn't want them to go in there and was happy when they went toward the kitchen. Stepping back into the empty living room, I was pretty sure that I, alone, had already collected enough evidence for Gabe and his group to keep their Internet celebrity going for years.

I wasn't sure what else we needed to do except to get rid of our ghostly residents since I had all the evidence I needed.

After giving the living room one last look, I went into the dining room to find Alyssa, Gabe, Mike and Smith all leaning in toward the monitors.

"It's like a giant screaming head," Alyssa said with the same expression one had when they passed a dead skunk on the side of the road.

"Did you hear it?" I asked, coming around to look at the monitors. A giant face appeared in front of me on the couch and yelled something inaudible and they could see the wind through my hair as I went back into the couch.

I rewound my tape and let the four of them listen. The final sound was a man's voice yelling, *"Katherine!"*

Smith was still skeptical. He gave Mike a doubtful look and shook his head. "What about our tape?"

Mike shrugged, rewound the recorder, and hit play.

"Here ghosty, ghosty…" Smith's voice came off as sarcastic.

"We should shove the fat one down the stairs," a whisper said into the tape. Then there was laughter.

"Stop it," a woman's voice said.

"Did you die in this house?" came Mike's question into the voice recorder.

"Of course we did. We all died in the house. In the basement," the first male voice whispered.

"The ring returns now," came a second male voice. "But Daniel, he won't leave."

"He can't," the first said. "It's his fault."

That was all their recorder had on it.

I shuddered. That was the same spirit I'd seen in the foyer. He'd said the same thing there. *He won't leave.* The spirit Daniel. The one who seemed to be keeping the other three here.

My mind raced with the riddle. I said aloud almost absently, "When is a ring not a ring? Or maybe the question is - when is a ring not a thing?"

Mike narrowed his eyes as if he'd thought the same thing. "What if the ring was a group of people? Maybe the leader killed them all in the house. In the basement."

"That doesn't make any sense," Alyssa scoffed. "Why would he ask Liz if she had the ring? Why would she have a group of dead people?"

Smith yawned and opened his beer. He took a swig. After he swallowed he asked, "Why do you care what the ring is?"

"Because it's the key to get rid of the spirits in the house," Alyssa told him squarely. She had little patience for non-believers. With a mad dash for her purse, she pulled out her phone and a pad of paper. "So what is the definition of a ring?"

Before any of them could answer, she'd queued up the answer on her phone. "So, a ring can be a piece of jewelry, or a disk, or circular item. A thing made of something else to encircle something. Right? Or, it can be a group of people with similar interests. Or it can simply mean to encircle something."

"I suggested a magick circle right before the ghost Daniel screamed Katherine," I reminded them. It was a nagging suspicion. "Maybe it's not a physical ring at all. Maybe a metaphysical one."

Alyssa got a bright, brimming smile on her face. "Ah! And what do we use rings for in magick?"

"To contain things, or for protection," I said, my voice trailing off.

"You did a protection on the house." That self-assured smile on Alyssa's lips grew bigger.

Mike put up a hand. "Wait, so you're saying that because Liz did a protection on the house, it somehow activated this *ring*, which activated the ghosts?"

"Something like that. What if the ghosts in the house were trying to protect it from something when they died, and your ghosts running through the house into the basement are trying to protect it again?"

"From what?" Mike and Smith exchanged glances.

"Maybe we need to take a trip to the historical society and find out who lived here and what they were so afraid of," Alyssa suggested.

I nodded. "Sounds like a plan, but it will have to wait until Monday. I can leave work a little early."

Shortly thereafter, other members of the team filed into the dining room to turn in their recorders. None of them caught a single thing, but Gabe was still happy with the evidence we did gather. By the time everyone left it was two in the morning and the house was silent. Gabe and his friends did a great job removing all of his cameras without leaving a single mark on any of the walls, and Mike's friends left still skeptical as ever, insisting we were playing a Halloween prank. We both fell into bed exhausted.

Sunday nothing happened. Not a damn thing. Mike put up shelves while I finished peeling off the old floral wallpaper. That evening, we painted the study and decided to let the paint dry and cure for at least two days before bringing in the cheap oak laminate bookshelves.

"Maybe we should invest in some quality bookcases at some point in the future. Real oak," Mike suggested. His eyes traveled to the moulding on the ceilings. Everything about the room looked regal and we both knew that the cheap bookcases wouldn't do it justice.

Mind you I'm not one to keep up appearances. I'm relatively low maintenance. But we bought the big *fuck-you* house. The least we could do was fix it up as nice as we could. It would do the house and the ghosts in it justice.

I don't know if the ghosts knew what we were doing, but they left us alone Sunday night, too. It was Monday morning, early, when they started getting impatient. The first thing they did was turn off the television. Then the hot water heater.

Finally, as both Mike and I dressed for the day, still chilled from cold showers, we heard the voice outside our door clear as a bell. "Do you have the ring? Elizabeth! Michael! The ring!"

Mike, with his service pistol drawn, went into the hallway, "Get down!"

I dropped, then realized he thought he was talking to a perp. Disembodied voices were a bit more disconcerting than your average cold spot, footstep, or floating specter. Especially when it sounded like there was a flesh and blood person behind it. Perhaps there had been, once.

"There's no one here," he called out to me from the hallway.

"I could have told you that," I said, straightening with caution. I took a deep breath and relaxed when Mike

71

returned, his gun in its shoulder holster. He put on his suit jacket. It's what he wore to work every day.

He came over and pulled me to him, kissing me square on the lips. "I love you."

"I love you, too. I am leaving work early to stop at the historical society with Alyssa, and then I'm going grocery shopping. I think I'll bring home a baked chicken from the deli." I know the last part likely wasn't what he wanted to hear, but it was as close to home cooked as he was getting for the foreseeable future.

He took it. "That's a step up from drive-through chicken any day."

Kissing me again he shook his head. "I hope you find something in historical records, because you're right – this," he motioned toward the door and the disembodied voice, "…isn't going to work. That is freaky shit, babe."

"We always succeed in solving the mystery, don't we?" I gave him a broad smile.

He nodded. "I suppose we do."

"It's because we're a good team," I ventured, pleased when he nodded again. This time I kissed him. "Have a really great day at work today. Be safe, okay?"

"You too." With that we both headed downstairs and out the front door. Another kiss and more goodbyes and we went our separate ways, both likely stopping at Starbucks for coffee since there was none in the house. Or at least I stopped. A mocha latte was exactly what I needed to get my head in the game.

I left the office at three and found Alyssa already inside talking to one of the historians.

"I know that house," the man was saying. "Beautiful restoration on the outside done by the last owner. They were here to get information to make it as historically accurate as they could. I think they were house flippers because they didn't own it long."

He dug through a cabinet and pulled out a file. "Built in 1897, but completely renovated in 1953. The wiring was updated back in 1992, and then the outside almost completely overhauled just last year."

"Well we're redoing the bathrooms this year and the kitchen has been totally renovated, but that was done by a previous tenant," I added.

"This is my friend. One of the new owners of the house. Liz Tanner," Alyssa told him with a big smile.

"Ah, Ms. Tanner. Alyssa was just telling me you were interested in the historical residents of your home." He smiled and set the file he had on the table between us. Opening it, he found what he was looking for. "So you're looking for a Daniel and a Katherine?"

"Yes," Alyssa said, taking charge like she always did.

"Here it is. Daniel and Katherine Smythe owned the house from 1912 to 1930." He shifted through the file again and produced some copies of newspaper clippings. "They did die in the house along with two other men. Daniel's brother Robert, and his friend Luke Penault. The authorities thought that maybe they had done something in the basement and perhaps tapped a natural gas vein, which ended up poisoning them. They found the basement windows blown out, and three bodies in the empty basement, in a circle. It appeared the cause of death for all four was asphyxiation according to the coroner."

The man stopped as if he was suddenly unsure he should be telling us this. "I hope this doesn't upset you…"

I let out a sigh. "No, I already know the house is haunted."

He let out a nervous laugh.

Alyssa joined him. "Liz is such a kidder. What we're really interested in is if there are any local legends about how they died. Or if there were any local legends that these four thought they would need to protect themselves from."

"You mean like the o-ccult?" the man said, placing plenty of emphasis on the *o* and saying it like *oh*.

I bit my lip to keep from laughing.

Alyssa couldn't hide her amusement. "Well, things like that or even legends of aliens or monsters, like chupacabra or bigfoot."

Now it was his turn to be amused. "Well, I don't know about any of that, but you can go down to the library and research it. I've never heard of bigfoot around here."

I laughed. "Is there any way we could get copies of that article?"

"It will cost you two dollars."

"Oh, absolutely. Also, do you happen to have blueprints?" I asked, digging two dollars from my purse and handing it to him. It was an expensive copy, but I wasn't going to argue.

We followed him to the copier. He set the paper on the glass and pressed the big green print button. "Yes. What are you looking for there?"

"I just want to see how much the structure of the house has changed or if it's stayed relatively the same." I flashed him a sincere smile. At least I hope it was sincere since it was becoming clear to me that there wasn't much else we could get from this guy.

He handed me the copy of the newspaper article, put his original back in the folder, then put the file folder back into the cabinet it came from. "Hold on a few minutes. I'll have to go into the other room for the blueprints."

Once he was gone I sighed at Alyssa. "I still have to go grocery shopping and this was a bust."

"I'll tell you what, I'll go to the library and see what I can find in the way of newspaper articles and obituaries, you go grocery shopping, and I'll call you if I find anything useful." Alyssa gave me a concerned look. "Are you okay?"

"Of course I am. We had a quiet weekend. Got the study painted. I think Wednesday I'll put the bookshelves in there and start unpacking the boxes of books." I stopped short when the thin, bird faced historian returned with blueprints.

"Here we are," he said, unrolling the blueprints on the table.

Both Alyssa and I looked them over. Everything looked the same, except in the blueprint there was a well to the east of the house, and below that, a well room accessed by the basement. But there wasn't a well room there now.

"It was common for wells to be filled in and old rooms like that bricked up once they were no longer needed," the historian told us, excited to share even the slightest tidbit of information with us.

"Thank you so much for all of your help." I shook the man's hand and waited for Alyssa to say goodbye, then we made our way back out to the parking lot. It was only four-twenty.

"So I'll call you from the library then. What's the date on that article?"

"October 5, 1930," I said, then added. "I would feel bad if you spent the next few hours at the library alone."

"Don't sweat it. Gabe has a meeting with a client about some software over dinner. Besides, I need a new book to read. I'll check one out while I'm there." She gave me a hug. "Love you and see you later Liz."

"Love you too, Liss. Thank you!" I went back to my car and watched as Alyssa pulled out of the parking lot, her sunny personality beaming from her smile. She was the happiest Satanist in the history of Satanists. I was sure of it.

The grocery store was a madhouse and by the time I got home, I found Mike sitting on the couch with a beer, flipping through the cable channels.

"There's nothing on."

"*Liturgy for the Dead* is on BMN," I said, carrying two heavy bags into the kitchen. "Or you could help me carry in the groceries."

"Did you park in the driveway?" He stood up and started toward the front door.

"Yeah. I wasn't carrying all that from the street."

Without word, he went out and began bringing groceries in while I stayed in the kitchen and put them away. My phone rang just as I finished putting the last of the frozen items in the freezer. Mike had the table set for dinner and was just getting ready to dig into the roasted chicken.

It was Alyssa. "Go ahead and eat," I told him, then answered. "Hey Liss."

"I think I just found the solution. You have to hear this. I'll be there in a few minutes." She sounded excited and ended the call before I had a chance to respond. Didn't anyone say goodbye anymore?

"Alyssa is coming by with her library research," I told Mike, who gave me a questioning look over a mouthful of chicken. "The historical society only knew how Daniel, Katherine and the others died. They think it was a natural gas leak, from the well or something. They were all asphyxiated."

He nodded. "Remind me to install all the carbon monoxide detectors and go through the basement with the gas leak detector just to make sure we're okay."

"Didn't we have the inspection guy check all of that?"

"Yeah, but ghosts are notorious for killing people like that." He said it with such authority, I almost believed him.

"No they don't."

"They could though." He grabbed a dinner roll from the packaged and opened a stick of butter.

Alyssa breezed into the house without knocking. At least she closed the front door behind her. "So get this – Katherine Smythe was a medium and every October she would hold séances here in the house. Upstairs actually. Her husband, Daniel, was a believer, too. So when she said she'd opened a portal to the other side and they began seeing wraiths, they became the laugh of the town. The local paper has an article about it the year before they died."

She handed me a copy of an article. I read the headline aloud. "Local medium predicts town will be over-run with wraiths this Hallow's Eve. Wraiths? Is that a real thing? I thought that was just a Scottish word for ghost."

Alyssa shrugged. "People back then believed weird things. Anyway, I looked and we were in a Saturn Scorpio transit back then. If Katherine was a strong medium and indeed opened a portal, they may have tried to create a circle of protection around the house to keep the spirits out. But somehow she didn't close the portal. What if that portal let something in, it killed all of them, and was so strong it blew out the windows?"

Mike finished his roll and said, "You're right. People back then believed really strange things."

I snickered and Alyssa rolled her eyes. "Just hear me out – it explains everything. We're in another Saturn Scorpio transit right now. So their tethered spirits think they need to build the protective circle again."

"Does that mean the portal is still open?" Mike asked.

"Possibly," Alyssa said. This time she didn't sound so sure of herself.

While the information she'd unearthed was interesting, I wasn't sure how it was going to help, but then I got an idea and it didn't involve the Demonic. Not entirely anyway. Just a little revealing spell. Sure, I could check with Demons every time something happened, but that seemed outright ridiculous. Instead, I often preferred to try to figure things out on my own, then seek Demonic intervention if things weren't working out.

I decided to share my plan. "How about I do a revealing spell? That should show us any open portals, we close any that are open, then we ask the spirits to move on, and finally we erect the protections. Problem solved."

"Why didn't we just do that to begin with?" Mike asked, this time sounding annoyed. "We went through all this crap when we could be done with it already."

He had a point. Had I thought of it sooner, I would have done it earlier, though admittedly I did want to know the history of the house. It brought the ghosts to life for me. I felt I understood them better. Besides, at least now we knew we were looking for portals.

"After dinner," Alyssa said, sitting down to eat. There was enough for her, too.

I smiled and joined them. The ghosts could wait until after dinner.

We took our time eating and finished right at seven. The house stood quiet against the night and a full moon filled the sky. By the time Halloween rolled around it would be a new moon – perfectly black pitch save for street lamps and candle lit pumpkins. I made another mental note that I needed to carve the pumpkins the coming weekend and put out Mr. Bones, my Halloween skeleton eight years running.

"So, what do you need me to do?" Mike asked.

I decided to give him an easy job, something that would keep him from the front line of spirit attack. "So when I do the revealing spell, you and Alyssa can just follow me while I close any portals, then after that we should remove the spirits, which will be Alyssa and I, and then you can help me smudge and anoint the entire house. You smudge, Alyssa will anoint, and I'll go through casting the warding symbols on every door and window to keep everything out. Let's hope there aren't open cracks to portals everywhere."

"*Everywhere?*" Mike repeated.

"I have a suspicion that if Katherine was a genuine medium, she likely had one foot in this world and one in the next, meaning portals likely opened randomly around her. If Daniel and Katherine weren't religious in a metaphysical way, the portals were never closed. Which means they've been open for eighty-five years or more."

"Well, I doubt there are many if there are," Alyssa said with a shrug.

"Why?" asked Mike. He narrowed his dark eyes.

Alyssa smiled. "Because the only spirits that seem to be haunting the place are the four who died here. Usually when you have open portals you have others, and they're far nastier, more violent, and scarier overall."

Mike gulped but didn't say anything.

Just because we hadn't seen the others yet, didn't mean they weren't already here. We'd only been in the house six days. "This house seems to have new owners every few years," I said, thinking aloud.

"There were exactly sixty owners including you and Mike after Daniel and Katherine died," Alyssa offered.

"There you go," I said, shrugging at Mike who cringed at such a high number. "It doesn't mean there aren't others here. Maybe we just haven't seen them yet."

"I'm surprised this place didn't just stay empty," he said, looking around. There was absolutely nothing menacing about the place until the spirits showed up.

"It's a charming house," Alyssa said in an upbeat tone. "You don't just pass on this much charisma and let it fall into disrepair."

I had to agree. Most of the time, the house's charm outweighed the spooky, unless you were superstitious. Honestly, I wouldn't have minded living in a haunted house if the ghosts were more polite and not as disruptive. "So let me run up to the boxes in the temple and find what I need."

"I'll come with you," Alyssa said.

Mike bit his lip. "I'd turn on television but there's nothing except horror movies, re-runs of old shows, and cooking competitions on. I guess I'll come too."

Together, the three of us went up to the still boxed temple so I could get the grimoire with the revealing spell in it, the wand I would need to seal any open rifts and create the wards, the anointing oil, and the smudge stick and bowl.

If my life were a Hollywood movie, there would be skulls, horned headdresses, a fog machine, and backlighting involved. But the reality was the spells and rituals were rather easy and relied heavily on visualization and projecting one's internal will. The only scariness I found myself concerned about was the potential for the physical manifestation and subsequent attack from spirits. All of which could accompany a potential resistance at closing the portals. I knew from experience that sometimes the *things* on the other side didn't like having their doorways deleted.

It made the most sense to begin the revealing spell in the attic and work our way down. That way we wouldn't miss any open portals in any part of the house. The Daemonic invocation felt strong and barbarous, leaving my tongue like the sharp edge of a blade, punching into the flesh of silence, and slicing the staleness of inert energy. An energy held solid in an unassuming pallor of arid death. Eighty-five years or more it sat there, filling the house. Tonight it would end.

I felt the air around me move, flowing toward something. A thing that sucked the life from the house. Likely a portal. There was definitely one here. Now it was just a matter of finding it. I could tell Mike and Alyssa felt it, too. It caused the senses to perk up, become aware. It stimulated the human instinct of flight or fight. Most people would flee, but we weren't most people.

Room by room we searched for it, and by the time we reached the main floor, I could feel the first one. Right there, in the study, it glowed a brilliant blue. A fissure between worlds that appeared almost as a crack in the fabric of reality. It pulled me as I imagine it pulled at Alyssa. I wasn't sure if Mike felt it, too, or if he was immune to its power.

Standing before it I took a deep breath and lifted the wand. I imagined the electric blue energy folding in on itself, back onto the plane of its existence, then carefully I pulled together the seams of the fissure, tighter and tighter. Drawing the wand, I pushed a pulsating violet light from my core, through my hand and into the wand. Now amplified and concentrated, the wand directed this metaphysical patching energy onto the crack between worlds, sealing it tight. It took almost ten minutes, and when I was satisfied I'd closed it completely, I took a deep breath and turned to Alyssa who gave me a nod of approval.

We continued through the main floor, not finding others, but we could feel the big one, reaching out to us from the basement.

While the portal in the study had been a quiet one, easy to fix, I knew the one in the basement would be an issue. Just a gut feeling. It felt twice as big, even from the kitchen.

"What have you done?" a male voice asked from somewhere around us. Even with the lights on, I felt the hair on my arms rise along with the chill on the back of my neck.

Mike heard it too. "Is there another one?"

"In the basement," I said, then added, "When that one is closed, we need to go through the house again to make sure nothing else popped open. Maybe even check the yard and the garage."

I wasn't taking any chances.

"To the basement," Alyssa said, fearlessly stepping in front of me and leading the way.

It was far bigger than I expected. It sat in the middle of the floor, hovering about four feet off the ground. I saw the figures of the house's ghosts cowering in the shadows, probably wondering how we were going to manage it. The revealing spell had activated each portal, bringing it to life.

"Should I open the windows?" Mike asked, and then reasoned, "Replacing them is expensive."

"Yeah, go ahead and open them," I said, not caring if the furnace had to work a little harder to combat the chill autumn air. Then I turned and addressed the spirits. "The problem working with spirits when you don't know what you're doing is you end up with portals."

Not that a lecture would do them any good now. That's when it dawned on me why all four of them were still there. Guilt. It wasn't their untimely deaths or their spiritual practices keeping them tethered to this world. No, they felt guilty for opening a portal they couldn't close and they felt responsible enough that they'd all been trying to protect the residents of the house from whatever was using this portal to step into the physical world. Whatever it was, it had killed all four of them. What remained of the ring pulsed as a faint red glow on the ground around the portal. A circle of protection. They'd attempted to erect a barrier.

A feeling of dread washed over me. I didn't share this with Alyssa or Mike because it was better off if only one of us feared the possibility of death. Instead, I closed my eyes, took a deep breath, and began the same process to close this portal.

An icy hand reached out from the fissure and gripped my throat. I felt myself choking, dropping the wand. It clattered to the floor, the echo of it clamoring noisily off of the cement walls.

I heard shuffling and Alyssa yelling something. Then I saw what it was in the portal. The thing appeared made of fire and air, its eyes mere slits of black, its grin violent and menacing. It sucked the air from me, drawing me toward the portal further. I could feel my consciousness draining from me, but I fought to resist.

In my mind's eye I drew that same violet energy from my center, but this time instead of pushing it through the wand, I built it up, then blasted it from every pore and appendage, knocking the *other* back onto the other side. I fell back, gasping for air, feeling the cool autumn night drifting in from now open windows.

Mike helped me back up. "Are you okay?"

I didn't answer him. "Give me the wand," I said to Alyssa, focused and determined.

She handed it to me, standing back.

I felt the violet energy build within me again, this time shoving it through the wand while simultaneously drawing the edges of the portal fissure together. I could see the thing trying to get its unearthly appendages through what remained, but I gave it a good mental shove, throwing it back. An icy blast of air erupted from the crack, sending a powerful gust of wind throughout the room. I was glad Mike had opened the windows – they would have shattered under that pressure I was sure of it.

Finally, I could pull the fissure tight. I applied the violet light to what remained, sealing it. When I was satisfied it was closed, I looked over at Alyssa who appeared exhausted, and realized she'd been helping me. It took both of us to close it.

"You okay?" she asked me, obviously shaken up.

I nodded. "Yeah. Did you see that?"

"No, but I felt it and I saw it strangling you and pulling you toward the portal." She looked back at Mike. "Good call on the windows."

"Yeah," he said, looking confused. "Are we done with portals?"

"We'll need to do another run through the house, the yard, and the garage, but if it's clear, yeah." Then I turned my attention back to the ghosts, who seemed almost anxious to know if everything was going to be okay.

I didn't say anything to them, and Alyssa only gave them a brief glance. We went back through the house, searched the yard, and the garage for more portals. Upon finding nothing, we returned to the basement. The ghosts had gone back into hiding.

"Katherine, Daniel," Alyssa called. "It's time for you to leave now. You no longer need to protect this house. We can protect it. Once you leave, we can put proper protections in place to keep the portals from coming back. But you have to go, or you'll be trapped here."

Slowly we saw their shadows emerge from the dark edges of the basement, never fully stepping into the light.

I heard Mike shift uncomfortably behind me.

"It's time for you to go. Thank you for letting us know the portals were here. We appreciate your warning and help," I said, hoping the spirits knew I was sincere.

One by one, each spirit vanished, except Katherine. I could see the long white nightgown, even in the dark corner that she hid herself in. "I will be watching over you," she said.

I heard the smile in her voice and watched her vanish into nothing. The heaviness lifted, and the brisk air of the room felt alive. Even the lights seemed brighter. One by one we closed the windows. Starting with the basement we established the wards, clearing out what was left of the old energy, and drawing Daemonic presence into every room.

By the time we were finished the house felt better. Warmer, more inviting. I breathed in the joy of our new home and knew that from that night forward, now that the ghosts of the house had been laid to rest, we'd sleep well.

FINIS

When Good Angels Go Bad
OTS # 4.7
(Read between Rocky Mountain Haunt and Illuminated
Darkness)

I always love the holidays at home, and by home I
mean Colorado, with my friends. Don't get me wrong, I love
my family, but the holidays in Arizona just aren't the same.
Back home it's too warm, my mom frets in the kitchen like a
chicken with its head cut off, my father watches football or
something equally vapid on television, and I'm stuck setting
the dinner table – bored and warm, longing for snow. It's just
not winter without snow.

This year I got lucky. My parents decided to go to my
uncle's in Georgia and I politely bowed out and decided Mike
and I would be celebrating with his mother, which is partly
true. The reality was that Alyssa, Gabe, Mike and I were
planning a huge holiday bash at the local Masonic Temple. A
Yuletide Ball replete with formal attire, black tie, and a solar
ritual in honor of the Daemon Belial. All of the
Daemonolaters, Satanists, and *Dark* Pagans along the front-
range had been invited, and so far we had one-hundred-

seventy-one RSVPs. The number was still climbing since the response cut off was still a week away.

I'd put Alyssa and Gabe in charge of the catering since Gabe's sister ran a huge catering company. Naturally Mike was in charge of security, and I took it upon myself, along with my co-workers at the *Black Magick Network*, to orchestrate the ritual, which we'd be broadcasting live for our viewers.

There was a light knock on my office door and Lamont Catrell, our resident alchemist, poked his head in. "Good Morning Liz. How you doing?"

I frowned at my computer screen. "Programming. Kirk wants me to replace *Dark Meditation* with *Daily Evocation* for *Evocation Week* in March, but if I do that on March fifteenth with these three episodes, Sorath, Kasdeya, and Zagan - we're opening a hell mouth somewhere and starting the apocalypse. I'm not so sure that's a smart idea."

Lamont chuckled. He got my snarky sense of humor. "Beware the Ides of March?"

Laughing, I peeled my eyes off of the monitor and smiled at Lamont, who'd become one of my favorite co-workers, and not just because he was easy on the eyes. No, he was the first real hardcore alchemist I'd ever known and we could talk magick and alchemy for hours. His show was my favorite in our lineup. "Something like that. How are you?"

"Getting psyched about your Solstice Ball. I have a date!" He came into my office and closed the door behind him. He set his *I'll-turn-you-into-a-toad* coffee cup at the edge of my desk and took the chair across from mine. "Her name is Lilith."

"Ah, the Daemon goddess…"

He nodded. "I can't say she's as serious as I am…magickally speaking."

His voice trailed off. I knew exactly what he meant. While my boyfriend Mike was an observant Daemonolater, he wasn't always practicing. I shrugged. "That seems to be how it goes though. Every pagan couple I know, there's one who observes while the other actively practices. It's the nature of the beast."

"Hmm." Lamont considered it for a second. "I think you're on to something. You know, if you and I had met only a few years earlier..." He gave me a wink.

I laughed again, trying not to blush. He often joked about what I'd thought a thousand times since I met him. If I hadn't been with Mike, Lamont and I might have ended up together – a magician power couple in a house constantly active with magick. While I still found that idea intriguing I knew deep down it would never happen. Not only was I happy with Mike, but two strong, ambitious, high achieving magicians in one household just wouldn't work. It couldn't. Magicians are egotistical assholes. I should know. So for now, I was just happy we were friends.

"So you're working on March?"

I nodded

"Am I still on the schedule?"

Lifting an eyebrow, I looked at my computer screen. "Yes. You haven't been cancelled yet."

"Good. Of course it's *only* December." He looked at his watch. "I actually stopped by to ask if you would mind meeting a friend of mine after work today. She needs some help and I thought of you..."

"Oh?" I was no longer feeling as flattered by his flirting. Everyone who knew me knew how much I hated being volunteered for things, especially since I was in the midst of planning the biggest event I'd ever planned.

"It's kind of a weird situation and I don't know what to make of it, but I know you deal with strange things all the time. Do you have time? Like maybe a half hour?"

I have to admit, I was intrigued, and it was only a half an hour. "Yeah, okay. I'll have to double check with Mike to make sure we didn't have anything going on tonight, but we'll plan for it."

"Thanks, Liz, you're great! I suppose I should get downstairs to the set. It's show time in an hour."

I gave him a smile and glanced back at the schedule on my screen. That's when I realized that I was fretting over March programming and it was only December fifth. "See you later Lamont."

"Later Liz." He exited the office with a bold greeting to Laura in the office next door.

I shook my head, got up, and began preparing for the morning production meeting.

Six o'clock seemed to come faster than usual. I called Mike to let him know I'd be late, which was fine with him since it gave him an excuse to go have a beer with some of the guys from work at Smokey's, one of the local cop-detective hang-out joints downtown. It was nice having a relationship where we could do our own things without the other becoming suspicious or jealous.

Closing my office, I made my way downstairs to the set of *Alchemy of Da'ath* to find Lamont chatting up one of the women on the camera crew. The young blonde blushed furiously, but her smile abruptly subsided when I showed up. That's often how it worked. The higher up you were, the fewer friends among the crew one seemed to have. Some days it sucked being the Director of Programming.

We agreed to meet at Marksman Brewery in a suburb directly west of Denver. When I got there, Lamont was already there with his friend, at the front door, waiting for me. He must have known a short cut because he looked like he'd been sitting there for a while. Of course with Lamont you never knew. He always seemed calm and collected regardless of what was going on around him.

"Kim, this is Liz, Liz – Kim," he said, introducing me to the thirty-something bottle blonde with a short, sassy cut. She towered almost a foot over me and was thin as a rail. A stark contrast to my own short athletic build and currently auburn hair with magenta streaks.

"It's so nice to meet you," she said, her blue eyes sparkling with what appeared to be relief.

Taking the hand she offered, I shook it. She was one of *those*. The type of person who had a limp handshake that made you not really trust them all that much. I forced a smile. "Likewise."

I was about to ask her about her situation when Lamont ushered us inside. It only took a few minutes for the hostess to seat us and we were immediately accosted by a server named Peter who wanted us to try the new IPA on tap.

"Just bring me whatever you have in a stout," I said.

Peter mumbled something about a milk stout, I nodded, and Lamont and Kim gave him their drink orders.

I wasted no time getting down to business. "So Lamont tells me you have a situation."

"Well, he tells me you work with Daemons," she started carefully.

"Yes. Daily." Of course it was a smug response. Magicians are assholes and I am, at my core, the quintessential magician.

Kim leaned in toward me from across the table. "This is kind of a delicate situation and we haven't involved the police because we were afraid it would raise suspicion."

My eyes widened. Immediately wishing my beer would arrive I swallowed a witty comeback and just listened.

"We were doing a standard evocation of angels. Our Seeress, Lynn, was sitting in front of the black mirror like we've done a hundred times before." She stopped short as our server arrived with our beer.

I immediately took mine and swallowed a mouthful. *Mmm, good beer.* There, that was better. A little.

Once the server was gone, Kim continued. "It was strange this time though. It was like the mirror turned to black liquid and Lynn went into a trance. We heard a voice say something we couldn't really make out. Like a hissing whisper beckoning her toward it. She stood up, and walked into the mirror and the rest of us just stared after her in shock. It was Brandon who finally took a few steps forward and put his hand on the mirror only to find it was solid. But we all saw it. Lynn literally got up and walked straight into the black mirror. We don't know how to get her out. We thought you might have some ideas."

That's when I realized my jaw was hanging open slightly. I took a deep breath. What did someone say to such a fantastical story? Besides, we were talking angels and angels were benevolent, for the most part. "Now, were any of you taking any psychedelic substances? Or were you under the influence of alcohol and drugs?"

It was the natural first question, especially since marijuana was now legal in Colorado. It seemed everyone smoked it except me, or my significant other, Mike. Mike, being a police detective in Cherry Hills, did not partake and me - I could never stand the stuff.

Kim seemed to understand why I asked the question and took it in stride. She shook her head. "No. We don't allow any drugs or alcohol during group ritual. Especially during evocation. It would be far too dangerous."

"Is it possible someone in the group slipped you guys anything?"

Lamont's dark brown eyes traveled from me to Kim and back again, like someone who was watching tennis.

"No. This is the same group I've been working with for three years. No new members or guests and we've done this ritual at least twenty-five times in the past three years." Kim took a nervous drink of her light, gluten-free beer and made a face.

I almost made a face with her. Gluten-free beer was disgusting. I took another deep breath, then another mouthful of *real* beer. I wasn't sure I could help her, but it wouldn't hurt to try, and if I failed, I decided then and there that I would encourage them to contact the police. For all anyone knew, someone in their group, perhaps even Lynn herself, had drugged them all, and used the ritual as a way to disappear. Some people wanted to disappear from their lives, after all. Or, the entire story was a ruse by people with overactive imaginations, or worse -- a story to cover up a murder. Either way, it was a mystery and my curiosity was piqued. "Can myself and some friends come and check out the ritual space tonight?"

"Absolutely," Kim agreed. "And you can see the video."

My jaw dropped more pronounced this time. "You have this on video?"

She nodded in an *of course* way as if I should have known. "We record all of our rituals on video. The video didn't blink out or get distorted or anything. It's really freaky."

Lamont nodded. "I've seen the video."

"Shit," was the only word that came out of my mouth. "All right."

Kim handed me her card with an address scrawled in tight script on the back. "Just call me first before coming by so I know to be expecting you."

Then she pushed the gluten-free beer away in disgust, dropped a ten on the table, thanked Lamont and I, said something about picking up her kids from daycare, and got up and left.

I was left blinking in disbelief at Lamont. A slow smile spread across his face. "I told you..."

"This is pretty intense. I need to call Alyssa and Mike and see if they want to go over there tonight. I've got to see this..."

He nodded. "I knew this was right up your alley when I saw it. You have some rapport with angels, right?"

While my area of expertise centered on the denizens of the infernal, to me, Angels were just another type of divine intelligence and I'd done my fair share of angel evocation and scrying with angels. I didn't answer him, just nodded back.

Yeah – this was definitely my cup of tea.

When I got home I found Mike sitting on the couch in front of the television eating a cheeseburger from *Lenny's Burgers*. He had it turned to the science fiction channel. It looked like a campy horror film.

When he saw me he pointed to a bag on the table. "Dinner. Double bacon cheeseburger."

Feeling a little guilty that I hadn't thought to pick up dinner myself, I smiled at him. "Thanks."

After washing down a bite of burger with a soda he said, "What did *Lamont* want?"

He said *Lamont* in a rather accusing way. Mike didn't like Lamont, probably because Lamont had no issue flirting with me in front of Mike, and Mike took issue with that.

I went into the kitchen, grabbed a glass of water, and then grabbed the burger and some napkins from the bag. There were fries in there, too. I ignored them. "It was Lamont's friend, Kim. She's one of the facilitators of a local Golden Dawn order. They have a slight issue."

Mike rolled his eyes.

"No, listen. This is bizarre and you'll like it. There's a mystery. One of their members went missing during a scrying session with an angel. Stepped into the mirror. Poof. Gone."

He let out a chuckle and shook his head.

"That's not the best part."

"Let me guess? The angel showed up and gave them some kind of cryptic message?" Despite Mike's experiences with the supernatural since meeting me, he was still skeptical. Well, until he saw something for himself.

"No. They caught it on video. We were invited to go over and look over the temple where it happened and view the video footage." I settled down on the couch with the cheeseburger. "I was going to see if Alyssa wanted to come, too. I thought we could swing by there tonight. They're just off of Twenty-Third and Gossling."

"How do we know the video hasn't been screwed with?"

"We take a copy with us and you send it to your lab of people."

"It's not *my* lab. I can't just use the lab when I want to, Liz. You know that."

"But it's a missing person case."

"Yeah, out of my jurisdiction."

I frowned at him. "Doesn't anyone owe you a favor? Or can they do it in their off time and we can pay them?"

"Let's look at it first. If it seems legit, I'll see what I can do," he finally agreed.

"Thank you." I gave him a peck on the cheek then focused on devouring the bacon cheeseburger. Afterward, I called Alyssa, who was obviously bored since she said she'd be right over, and I called Kim to let her know we were coming over, assuring her we wouldn't be there longer than an hour or so.

It was eight-forty-one when we pulled up to the small, brick, single family home with a one car garage not too far from my old house. Kim sat out on the front porch smoking a cigarette. She appeared to be just finishing up.

We got out of the car and I nodded to her. "Hi Kim. Thanks for letting us come over tonight."

"I appreciate you coming," she said, her eyes darting over my shoulder to my companions.

I pointed to Mike, "This is my significant other, Mike. He's actually a detective, and this is my friend Alyssa who has helped out in other investigations," I explained, not wanting to go into too much detail.

"Are they practitioners?"

"Yep." Then I realized I hadn't introduced Kim. "Oh, and you guys, this is Kim."

Everyone nodded acknowledgement. I could sense Mike sizing Kim up, probably wondering if she had any reason to lie.

Kim put out her cigarette, a Winston light I noticed from the pack she carried with her, and opened the door to her house. "Come on in. Excuse the mess."

We followed her inside to a cozy living room decorated in earth tones. It was cluttered with a ball and some coloring books on the floor, a stray blanket left in a heap on the recliner, and some small shoes tossed carelessly in front of a closet door. Not really my definition of a mess. Not when people had kids. The living room flowed into the dining room where a man, not much older than Kim, stocky, with light brown hair and dark eyes, sat at the dining room table in front of a laptop. He looked up and acknowledged us.

Kim introduced us. "This is my husband Kevin."

Kim and Kevin, I thought, musing how they probably had kids named Kyle and Karen, or Katrina and Kasey. If I had been Megan or Melissa, Mike and I might have done the same thing, for the sake of symmetry and order. I decided not to be presumptuous and ask the children's names despite my curiosity. Besides, they were likely in bed already and an introduction was unlikely.

Kevin looked at the computer screen again, then at us. "I have the video cued up. Do you want to see it first? Or look at the temple first?"

Mike pulled out a chair next to him. "I want to see the video."

Alyssa nodded wordlessly and stepped up behind Mike. I did the same.

Kevin turned the computer screen toward us and clicked the play button. Then he sat back and watched our reaction.

When I heard the invocation the operator intoned, my hair stood on end. I watched, my eyes transfixed to the screen. The seeress stood up and stepped into the full length black scrying mirror, disappearing, just like something out of a science fiction movie. Then we saw a man step forward and touch the mirror, hitting a black surface.

"What the fuck," he said.

"This is a joke, right," said one of the participants.

"Oh my God!" It was Kim in the video. She ran around to the back of the mirror. "She's gone. Lynn's gone."

Then there was chaos, the lights turned on and people ran around the room looking in bizarre places for the missing seer with no luck. It appeared no one had closed the circle.

Mike regarded the video with that look he got when he was trying to figure something out, and he started to bite his lip. "Can I get a copy of this video?"

"Yeah, I have it uploaded to an online drive. I can share it with you and you can download it if you want. Or move it to your online drive," Kevin said.

Mike agreed and gave Kevin his email address. Thank the gods for modern tech. I could only imagine how a mystery like this would have been solved before video cameras and the internet. Then Kim led us through the kitchen, toward the back door, and down a flight of stairs into the basement.

At the bottom of the stairs she slipped a key into the lock, and with a twist and click, opened the locked door, and flicked on a light. I couldn't help but feel relieved to know they kept a lock on the temple, especially with kids running around. I stepped into the bright room. The entire finished basement had been turned into an enviable temple.

"Nice," Alyssa commented. It was the only thing my usually perky blonde Satanic friend had said since we arrived.

I immediately got a chill and stepped into what was obviously a holy place, noticing Enochian tablets, carefully painted, stood aloft on pedestals in their appropriate quadrants. The scrying mirror, a full length piece of glass painted black on the back, stood slightly right of center, near the tablet of union. On the floor was painted a carefully crafted circle that could be changed with chalk. Basically, the temple looked the same way it had in the video.

"You guys haven't changed it since she disappeared? And did anyone close the circle after it happened?"

Neither Kim nor Kevin answered.

Mike went over to the mirror and investigated it, while Alyssa spent time looking over the walls. Maybe for trap doors or something, I wasn't sure. When I started to move through the room, both of them stopped and looked at me, knowing I would likely see things they wouldn't. Being a medium, a genuine medium, isn't nearly as romantic as television and movies make it seem. Sometimes it's downright terrifying, no matter how used to seeing things you think you are. And whatever was in that temple wasn't good.

There was something there that scared the shit out of me. To be honest, I wanted to turn tail and run, but I forced myself to walk forward, toward the mirror.

"Elizabeth…" the voice whispered.

My blood ran cold. Son-of-a-bitch, I hated that. The spirits on the other side always knew more about me than I knew about them. At first. But I knew from experience that they'd eventually let me in on who they were and what they wanted – whether I wanted to know or not.

"Who are you?" I asked. I could feel Kim and Kevin's eyes on me from the doorway, and Mike and Alyssa watching me.

"Bataivah," the voice hissed. Then a cold wind blasted through the room from the East wall.

Son-of-a-bitch. Enochian spirits. Well, in all fairness they weren't just any spirits. They were, technically, angels, and not necessarily the benevolent kind. Of course most angels had a dark side, but there was something about Enochian angels that terrified a lot of magicians, myself included. Then I reminded myself that the only reason I was terrified was because the angels vibrated at a higher, more uncomfortable, for humans anyway, frequency. Didn't they? That's what created the scared feeling. Even as I thought it, doubt crept in. No, this was different. This wasn't just a vibration. These spirits had actually taken a human woman into their realm, but why?

I focused my attention on the mirror. "Bataivah, where is Lynn?"

The mirror began to fog and an image began to appear. Something compelled me to move forward, toward it.

Inside the mirror I saw a face without a nose and a mouth without lips. The eyes blazed yellow. "With us. Join us."

Against my will, my legs began moving toward the mirror. I couldn't look away from the face – those eyes.

Then I felt a strong arm around my waist, pulling me backward and I snapped out of the trance. The image of the face faded to nothing.

"Liz, stop," Mike whispered in my ear. "Breathe."

He sounded scared and I took a deep breath. "What the hell?"

"You were talking in some weird language."

"I got it on my phone," Kevin said from behind us. He stepped into the room and turned the screen toward us, tapping the *play* icon.

There, on the small screen I saw myself walking toward the mirror, saying something in what sounded like Enochian, the language of the angels.

"Write it down phonetically," Alyssa said, pulling a pad of paper and a pen from her inner jacket.

"No need," said Kevin. "That's a standard invocation of Bataivah without the signs and pentagrams."

"Are you sure?" Mike asked, giving me a strange look.

Kevin nodded. "I've done the same invocation at least once a month for the last five years. First you vibrate EXARP, Air of Spirit. Then you vibrate OROIBAHAOZPI, which is the secret holy name of air, then begin vibrating BATAIVAH, who is the King of air. It's always in that order."

The thing was, I hadn't worked enough Enochian magick to know this by heart, but I couldn't prove that I didn't know it.

"Did you do this invocation when Lynn disappeared?"

"Well, yeah. But I completed the entire evocation of the watchtowers, all of the elements, before we did the scrying session." Kevin seemed as perplexed as Mike was.

Me, I was too busy shaking off the foggy, surreal feeling overwhelming me.

"Can you send me *that* video, too?" Mike proceeded to give Kevin his cell phone number so he could just send it by text.

"We should go," I said. I turned to Kim. "I need some time to think about this and decide the next course of action and I'll call you."

I started back up the stairs, Mike close at my heels and Alyssa behind him. Kevin and Kim were the last to ascend the stairs after locking the door to the temple, and both looked a bit upset.

"These things take time to solve," I said apologetically. "That's... I... You..."

I wasn't sure what to say. They had something definitely freaky going on in their temple and I was still chilled to the bone by it.

Leading the way, I made a b-line for the door. As I left the house I said, "Don't let anyone in that temple. Keep it locked for now. I have a feeling one person wasn't enough."

"What do you mean?" Kim started after us.

"We'll call you," Mike said, the concern still clear in his voice.

I made my way out to the car, feeling on the verge of emotional collapse. I usually only had a negative reaction like this if I encountered something really bad. Yeah, it was bad. I blinked back some tears, got in the car, and closed the door.

Alyssa jumped in the back and put her hand on my arm. "Liz, what's going on? Are you okay?"

I wiped the tears away. "Enochian spirits have a different kind of energy, you know?"

"Bullshit." Alyssa knew me better than that.

Mike got into the car, closed the door, put the key into the ignition and looked at me with those beautiful dark eyes I fell in love with. "We're leaving."

Alyssa sat back into the back seat with a huff, knowing she wasn't going to get a straight answer from me, and buckled her seatbelt.

We were a few blocks away before I felt well enough to say anything. "Well that was awful."

"What happened back there?" Mike asked

"Enochian angels."

"That's not an answer," he said.

From the backseat Alyssa said, "Actually, it is. Enochian spirits are well known for being nasty. But isn't it something about vibration, Liz? In one of your books you said..."

"Not this time." I cut her off. "There's something bigger going on here. I just don't know what yet."

We were silent all the way home. Alyssa left after bidding Mike and I goodnight, and we soon found ourselves sitting in front of the television, watching both videos, which Mike had downloaded to his tablet and connected to the TV.

Over and over again we watched Lynn walk into the mirror, and then over and over again we watched me almost do the same thing. Finally, around midnight, Mike yawned. "I'll see if Max, at the lab, will look at the video of Lynn disappearing. As for you, Miss Medium, you need to stop going into these strange trances and freaking me out."

I gave him a tired pout. "I don't mean to. It just kind of happens sometimes."

"I think it's time for bed." He yawned again, looking at the clock. Then he got up and collected his phone and glass of water.

"I think I'm going to be up a little while longer."

Mike nodded, leaned over and kissed me, and said, "Don't stay up too late. You still have to work tomorrow."

"I won't." I gave him a weak smile.

Waiting until he was in bed, I pulled out a DVD of some magicians evoking the Enochian watchtowers. Popping it into the player, I sat back and watched, making sure the volume was low as not to disturb Mike. The entire ritual was actually quite beautiful in its construct. The colors and imagery all held deep meaning. Even the intoned evocations in Enochian, harsh as they were, sounded beautiful. When it was over I shook my head, not sure what I'd hoped to find by watching it. Maybe some clue as to what the angels wanted. No luck. I turned the television off and got up. It was time for bed.

There was nothing but blackness. Not a murky, shadowy blackness. No. This was absolute darkness. I felt myself surrounded and I was terrified. My body shook. They didn't say anything. I took a deep breath and sat there, naked to them. Vulnerable. They said nothing, just watched me. Their energy vibrated around me sending my senses and instincts into flight mode, but I forced myself to ignore it. I was helpless to them. Captive. I took my mind to a place where I could separate the fear I felt and look at these beings from an objective viewpoint. There, I found them curious, entranced by the mortal flesh that housed my immortal soul. Curious about what made me tick. Surely they knew. They were angels, after all. I could feel their minds probing mine, but they gave me very little to work with.

"Join us," one of them hissed. Then I felt a release, as if they'd allowed me from their grasp. I found myself suddenly back in my body and I shot straight up in bed, so sudden that Mike woke up alongside me.

"What's wrong?"

"Freaky dream."

Weary, he looked over at the clock on the bedside table. "About?"

"I was just astral-napped by a rogue band of Enochian angels."

He chuckled.

I was dead serious, but instead of saying anything, I settled back down into my pillow and tried to go back to sleep. It was no use. The experience shook me to my core, and when the alarm went off two hours later, I got out of bed and got ready for work as if nothing had happened at all.

When I arrived at the office I realized I hadn't remembered the drive there. So entrapped in my own mind, it felt as if I was floating through. I went straight to Lamont's small office downstairs. He was there talking to a few staff members who immediately cleared when I came in.

I closed the door before saying anything. "We need someone who knows the Enochian spirits far better than me."

"Easy – Gavin Windeck." He lifted an eyebrow. "You want to tell me why?"

"Last night I was astrally napped by some Enochian spirits."

Lamont didn't say anything at first, he just looked at me. Finally, he said, "Gavin Windeck doesn't like BMN, and my guess is he probably doesn't like you."

I frowned. Lamont was right. I wasn't popular among the serious ceremonial crowd, and neither were the risk taking, experimental, and often eccentric magicians of the *Black Magick Network*. Mostly, I was here for the job and because I knew the people. Good people who took their art seriously. Of course in the world of magick, everyone thinks they have the one-true-way and that no one else is as authentic as them. While I've always had a live and let live philosophy, Gavin Windeck did not. He was pretty sure the rest of us were frauds and only he knew what the hell he was doing.

"Anyone else?" I asked. Gavin Windeck was becoming less and less of an option.

Lamont shrugged. "You could always ask Luke Martin. He's a bit more open-minded and he could always approach some like Gavin without Gavin having to know you're involved. Luke's a friend of mine."

"Yeah, can you maybe call Luke on this?"

"You got it." Lamont smiled at me.

I could tell he wanted me to stay and give him more details, but I had a meeting in twenty minutes and to be honest, I hadn't fully been able to process the experience yet. I needed more time.

I didn't get to talk to Lamont the rest of the day and I headed home still wondering how I was going to help Lynn. The only solution I could think of came to me while I was sitting in the kitchen that evening making party favors for the ball, clay Belial sigil pendants. I'd have to invoke my allies in the angel world and ask them what to do about it. Just as I got up to go into the temple to do just that, my phone rang. It was Lamont.

"Bad news," he started.

I groaned. "Let me guess, your friend Luke refuses to help?"

"Actually, he's in Switzerland for the next month, but he had a suggestion."

"Yeah?"

"He suggested invoking one of the archangels and asking for help."

I bit the inside of my cheek. "That's not helpful. I was just going into the temple to do that. Uriel. I have a good working relationship with him, but... I have a bad feeling."

"Maybe you're just stressed with all this party planning. I'm going to make you an elixir to help you get through the holidays, girl." He sighed deeply into the phone. "Good luck with Uriel and I hope we can tell Kim something afterward? She called me earlier a little stressed out. She's really worried about Lynn."

"Likewise," I said. It was true, there wasn't an hour that went by where I wasn't thinking about Lynn. "My concern is she's been in there for more than three days now. Humans can't live three days without water."

The other end of the line was silent.

"Lamont?"

"Sorry, just, yeah. I hadn't considered the water thing. Do you think she's dead?" Lamont sounded nervous now.

"I don't know. I hope not." Of course in my heart there was a spark of hope. Psychically, at least, I knew she was still alive, but the clock was ticking. "Lamont, I have to go."

"All right. Call me when you're done?"

"Okay." I hung up. Mike was working late tonight so I had the house to myself, which was always a bonus for ritual work. While I didn't mind doing it when he was here, it was a lot easier and more efficient when he wasn't.

Our temple wasn't nearly as enviable as others I'd had the privilege to see. It doubled as an office slash guest room temporarily while we renovated and worked on a dedicated space. Something I could lock the door on when my parents came for a visit.

It only took me a few minutes to set up before I began my invocation to Uriel. The angel showed up promptly, this time in feminine form.

The angel didn't say anything. Instead, she just stood there, her presence overwhelmingly warm and energetically bright. That was the *Light of God* for you.

"I need you to help me find out what happened to Lynn and help me find a way to bring her back. A human has no place in your realm." I felt silly saying it, half expecting the angel to tell me to throw a twelve sided die.

Instead, Uriel unfolded her wings and stepped toward me. Then she opened her mouth and out from it came a loud melodic cry, her hot breath blasting my face. The angel then put her face next to mine, her gold eyes blazing into mine. I heard her speak in my mind's eye. "Those who seek the angels set the trap. Lynn is in the trap."

I forced myself to stay put and not move away. "How do I get her out? She can't live without water!"

Uriel laughed at me. "Silly child. She's in a state of stasis, she needs no water. Now go. Set the trap."

With that, Uriel vanished before me and I was standing alone in the temple again.

I took a deep breath once I realized I'd been holding it. A trap. A spirit trap?

Just what, exactly, had Kim and their coven been doing? I extinguished the candles in a hurry, and took up my phone, dialing Lamont.

"Liz!"

"Lamont! Call Kim and tell her I'm coming over. She and Kevin better be ready to tell me what the hell they were doing, because I wasn't getting the whole story. Tell her I know about the trap."

"The trap?"

I didn't answer him. Instead, I ran through the house gathering up my things.

"Liz? What trap?"

"Just call her." I hung up and called Mike, leaving a message telling him where I was going. I called Alyssa, too, who begged me to stop by and pick her up. She didn't want me to go alone. Before I left, I checked to make sure everything was off and the house was locked, then I went out to the garage to grab some copper wire and a crystal. I wasn't sure it would work, but I'd heard stories and I was willing to try anything.

I soon found myself heading toward Alyssa's. She was outside waiting for me and jumped into the car. I started toward Kim's.

"They were using a spirit trap to trap the angels, but angels aren't stupid," I said without waiting to catch her up. Instead, I continued with my rant...

"So the angels were like *Fuck this, we're going to teach you a lesson by taking one of your people.* So they did. They took Lynn. Now if they do another ritual in that temple – the angels will keep taking people. So I have a plan. I'm going to first dismantle the spirit trap in the temple and promise them that the coven won't do it again."

I must have sounded like a crazy woman because Alyssa was giving me a look that suggested as much.

It was no matter, I was on a roll. "Then I'll ask for Lynn back. If they don't hand her over willingly, I'm going outside, creating another spirit trap, and taking one of theirs that I'll use to exchange..."

"Okay, this is crazy. You're talking about kidnapping *an angel* and swapping prisoners? Are you fucking out of your mind?"

"Do you have a better plan?"

"Yeah! I say we do what you said and if they refuse to give her over, we contact an arch angel to make them comply." Alyssa shrugged. "Or we send a Daemon after their asses."

"I already talked to Uriel. She wasn't sympathetic. Basically – these guys deserve what happened. Maybe it will teach them to not screw with angels. Or any spirits for that matter." At a stoplight, I gave her a sidelong glance. "We don't want to start some kind of Daemonic war either. I can't imagine any of the other spirits, Daemonic or not, would be sympathetic to the use of magickal spirit traps either."

"I see your point," Alyssa agreed. "But you don't need to be pissing them off by trying to trap them either."

"I won't be."

"But you just…"

"No. I changed the plan – you're going to do it. But only if I need you to."

Alyssa's jaw dropped. "What?"

"I will dismantle the trap, get Kim and Kevin to promise never to do it again, get the angels to agree to let Lynn go, and then I'll go into the mirror to get her."

My best friend's eyes grew wider. "You've lost your mind."

"No, hear me out. If I can't get back out, you take the copper wire and the crystal outside and make a spirit trap…"

"This is the dumbest plan ever. And what the hell am I supposed to do with a crystal and copper wire?"

"You trap the angel in the crystal in a copper circle. It will keep it trapped."

She gave me another *look*. "Did you just make that shit up?"

I shook my head. "I don't think so. I read it somewhere."

"Seriously? You read it somewhere?" She sounded exasperated. "And if that doesn't work and you're both trapped inside the mirror? Then what?"

"I'm not the only magician on the planet. Talk to Lamont Catrell. He'll have some ideas I'm sure." We pulled up in front of Kim's house.

Again, Kim was waiting outside. This time Kevin was with her. It was still early, not quite seven-thirty.

They both looked guilty. Evidently Lamont had relayed my message.

I got out of the car and immediately asked, "Who constructed the trap?"

Kevin answered. "It was Brandon's idea. We thought it would be interesting to try it."

"We need to deconstruct it. I hope the kids aren't home?"

"They're at my mother's," Kim said quietly.

They both seemed ashamed of themselves, as well they should have.

Kim and Kevin led us back down to the basement temple. Beneath the mirror was a rug. I hadn't noticed it the first time.

He moved the mirror and pulled the rug aside, revealing a wooden disk with a copper sigil inlayed in it. He looked up at me. "We would have used silver, but it was too expensive. Copper is cheaper and it conducts electric fields better."

I looked at the sigil and shook my head. It was the same seal used on a popular television show, but the intent in its making and the placement had worked well enough. Enough to piss off a few angels who were now teaching this coven a lesson in humility among other things.

Of course now it was up to me to clean up the mess since I took Uriel's response to my invocation as a cry for help.

Kevin pulled the wooden disk from the ground, replaced the piece of carpet, and set the mirror back on it. He looked down at the sigil. "What do I do with this now?"

I shrugged. "Burn it? Actually, I'd remove the copper, recycle it, and then use the wood for kindling."

He nodded at me and handed the three foot by three-foot disk to Kim.

She took it. "I'll put it up in the garage so you can get the copper out of it."

Once Kim had left the room with the disk, I felt the energy in the room suddenly change. That was more like it.

"Oh, copper..." Alyssa remarked, now realizing why I'd grabbed a roll of copper wire for a spirit trap.

"So why did you guys do this?" I asked. To be honest, I wasn't sure why anyone would try to trap an angel, unless they were crazy or stupid, or watched too much television. Anyone who worked with angels knew that angels could be rather brutal when fucked with.

Kevin seemed to weigh his response carefully. "Brandon thought it might make for a stronger connection. We use it for Daemonic invocation, too."

Fighting the urge to roll my eyes I just said, "And you agreed."

No, it wasn't a question. I was simply being honest. One guy had the brilliant plan to try to get more spirits to appear in the mirror, or manifest to physical appearance, and everyone else agreed without thinking of the possible consequences. That's usually how it happened.

Kevin didn't say anything, just gave me a helpless look. That, of course, told me everything I needed to know. Kevin was easily led and it seemed Brandon, who had obviously disappeared when shit got real, was the one running the show. As well as the one who was absent when it came time to clean up the mess.

I turned to Alyssa. "All right. I'm going in. When I find Lynn, I will bring her straight out. If I'm not out within an hour, I want you to call Lamont and Mike, and as a last resort, you guys will have to build a spirit trap and try to trap an angel in the crystal."

Alyssa shook her head. "Do you even know if that will work?"

"Nope." I was doubtful. Really doubtful, but it was the only solution I could come up with, and no one else had offered an alternative. "Just remember your intent when making it. To trap an angel for a prisoner swap. Seriously."

"Fuck..." Alyssa was not happy. I could tell by the way she glared at me.

"I know, you're totally risking your karma for me, but I'd do the same for you. If you want, you can go in..."

"I believe you have already been introduced. I haven't. Besides, angels aren't really my forte. I'd probably burst into flames." She frowned. Her usually cheery demeanor was gone.

"Well, with any luck this will work..."

"And if it doesn't?"

"You'll have to cross that bridge when we get there. That's why I said you should call Lamont and Mike. I think between the three of you, you can figure something out." Evidently I had more faith in the three of them than Alyssa did.

She didn't say anything - just kept frowning.

I looked at Kevin who seemed okay with whatever we were doing. "Why don't you go call Brandon and have him come over. When this is done, I want to have a talk with the three of you."

Kevin looked surprised. "Okay."

Alyssa gave me a questioning look.

I didn't elaborate, but it didn't take a genius to figure out that I intended to give them all a good ass-chewing once I had Lynn safely back in this world. If I could get Lynn back and if the angels didn't decide to keep me, too.

Kim, having delivered the spirit trap to the garage for dismantling, came back down the stairs and into the temple.

"Everyone ready for nothing?" No one responded. They all just looked at me. I looked at Kevin. "Open the temple and call the watchtowers."

The surprised look in his eyes told me he hadn't expected me to say that.

"Is that a problem?"

"Uh, n-n-no," he stammered. As if I'd cracked a whip, he suddenly got very serious and set to work, constructing the ritual space and speaking the invocations, or evocations as he called them.

I didn't care what he called them as long as the angels showed up and opened the mirror to their realm so I could get in. I was all business when it came to magick.

When he finished his invocations I found myself standing in front of the mirror. Nothing was happening. "Don't tell me this shit isn't going to work without that damned spirit trap..."

My mind raced to the possible implications that the copper energy conduit was necessary to open the portal.

Alyssa interrupted my thoughts. "Maybe you should invoke Uriel, then do the invocations of the watchtowers yourself..."

"Fair point." I waved Kevin off, out of my way. I stood in the center of the temple and took a deep breath, my arms raised. "'I invoke thee, Uriel to stand on my left. I have dismantled the spirit trap as you have requested. Please open the gateway to your realm that I may bring Lynn back to this world where she belongs."

I felt a slight rustle of air and heard a whoosh on my left side. The angel's presence filled the room. Then, in a brief panic I realized I didn't know the Enochian invocations by heart. I needed a book or something, but then I felt a warm feeling envelop me, and my body hummed to the energy of

Uriel. The words began to come from my lips as if I'd known them forever.

My feet carried me to the East, "ORO IBAH AOZPI BATAIVAH."

Then I moved to the North, "MPH ARSL GAIOL RAAGIOSL."

Over the West, "MOR DIAL HCTGA ICZHIHAL."

Finally, to the South, "OIP TEAA PDOCE EDLPRNAA."

My head felt fuzzy with euphoria and the world suddenly became surreal. I saw the glass of the mirror ripple like water as the portal opened.

"Join us," a voice hissed.

I couldn't say anything. It was as if my body was possessed and I had no control over my voice, or my legs. I felt my feet carry my body toward the mirror, completely oblivious to everything in the room. The only thing I had complete control over were my thoughts and so I projected my thoughts at the open portal. "I'm only coming in to take Lynn back."

"She is here," the voice hissed.

"I know she's there, that's why I'm coming in," I thought sarcastically.

Another angel snickered. Who says angels don't have a sense of humor?

Reaching the mirror, my hand reached up and touched the rippled glass, which vanished to steam, then clear air. I stepped inside the blackness, feeling a distinct difference in the energy around me. They were there, watching me. Curious and staring.

"How will I find anything?" I thought. My eyes were useless here, as was my nose, and my sense of taste. I could hear nothing. It was as if sound ceased to exist. However, I could think and I could feel their energy. Not on limbs or skin, but to the very core of my being. The energy vibrated in such a way that I felt consumed by it.

"Open your heart," another voice whispered. But it wasn't like I heard it. Instead, I felt the voice. It resonated in my thoughts like a song. Now I knew what it meant to hear angels sing. It was far deeper than just some distant auditory experience. No, it pulled you in, consumed you, and lifted your spirit.

Giving way to pure emotion, I followed, not knowing if I was moving or sitting still, or perhaps passed out on the floor of the temple in Kim and Kevin's basement. Nothing existed except my consciousness, and theirs, and that all-consuming darkness. Then I felt light. Not by warmth necessarily, but by compassion and vibrancy. Another living creature. I wondered then if this is how the angels felt us, as I was feeling Lynn.

"Yes," whispered a voice that vibrated like a C cord and then F.

My light merged with hers and I felt the weight of it, like stone. She was clearly unconscious. "I will need help to get her out."

"Be the light," the helpful voice sang at me.

The angels surrounded me. I could feel them, could feel their curiosity. I felt their gossamer wings caress my light. Focusing on carrying Lynn out, I imagined the portal and started toward it, but because I couldn't feel my body I had to imagine I had one, and that I was flying toward a bright light, back toward those I loved. Mike, Alyssa...

I didn't expect to catapult out of the mirror and dive to the ground gasping for air. Everything was still foggy and my head hurt in a miserable way. Lynn lay next to me moaning, even more incoherent than I was.

The blur that was Kim rushed to help Lynn up. I knew it was her because I could feel her. My own eyes had not yet readjusted to the light.

A strong arm lifted me up and steadied me on my feet. I couldn't focus, but I could feel it was Mike. Lamont was there, too. I could feel each of their separate energies. My legs felt spongy and it was a chore to get up the stairs. He helped me sit in a chair at the dining room table. Someone brought me a glass of water. I drank, and drank, and when the glass was emptied, Mike handed me another and I drank some more. After about ten minutes I could focus and I felt readjusted to this world.

"Why did you call Lamont and Mike? I was only in there for a few minutes."

"Try three hours," Alyssa deadpanned.

"You didn't have to create a trap?"

She shook her head. "No, but we were about to."

I looked around the table. Lynn and I sat at one end, and Alyssa and Kim sat across from us. Lamont, Mike and Kevin were standing. We all looked at each other. The doorbell rang.

"I'll get it," Kevin said. "It's probably Brandon."

"Good," I said, remembering I'd asked Kevin to summon him.

Alyssa gave me that questioning look again.

Lynn, so traumatized by the experience, seemed still in a daze.

"How are you?" I asked her.

"I'll be okay," she whispered, giving me a weak smile.

"You need food, water, and sleep. You should take it easy for a few more days. Did anyone contact your family or check on your pets or call into your job or anything?"

Lynn shrugged. "I live alone. No pets."

Kim cringed. "We didn't call your boss."

I bit my inner lip. Nice friends. Glad they weren't mine.

Brandon made a grand entrance, his arms open. "Lynn, we were so worried!"

Shaking my head, I looked at him in disbelief. "This is the first time I've seen you since I was called in to clean up your mess."

"You are?"

"Elizabeth Tanner."

Lamont pointed at me, "*The* Elizabeth Tanner, The Daemonolatress. Programming Director of the *Black Magick Network*."

Instead of a *hello* or even a snotty *fuck you*, he gave Kevin a look of derision. "You called in a demon worshiper?"

Kevin cowered.

"Someone had to come in and clean up the mess. And since I was the one who had to do it, you're all going to listen to what I have to say, and then I'm going to leave and never bother you again." I was good at laying things out like that.

Brandon glared at me, but didn't say anything.

"Good." I felt like I was speaking to an unruly school kid. "Experimentation is great, but you need to take more responsibility for your magick. From my understanding, the spirit trap was your idea, Brandon, and when it backfired, you disappeared, bailed on Lynn, and left your coven-mates, Kim and Kevin, to deal with it. They took it to Lamont, and Lamont contacted me. So I came in, as a favor to Lamont, and Lamont as a favor to Kim and Kevin - to clean up the mess *your* experiment made. You were nowhere to be found. So next time you decide to do something like this, and things go awry, maybe you should actively try to help clean up the

WITHIN DARKNESS | AUDREY BRICE

mess. If I'm called to clean up your mess again, I'm going to send Focalor after your ass."

The threat of Focalor didn't scare him, a sure sign he was an idiot. "Is that all? That's the reason you called me over here?"

"Yeah, that's all I have to say to you." Then I turned to Kevin, and Kim. "Seriously - you guys need to tell the coven what's acceptable and what isn't. Put your foot down. It's your house and your temple. Your rules. Personally, anyone in my group who showed the lack of responsibility Brandon here did, would be tossed out on their ear in a heartbeat. That's just a friendly piece of advice."

I turned to Lynn then, reached in my pocket, and pulled a business card from my wallet. "If you find you've lost your job since no one in your coven thought to call your job to let them know you'd be out, call me. I know of a few places hiring, though I don't know what it is you do. Regardless, I know people in just about every line of business."

Then I stood up. "It was nice meeting you all, I wish it had been under less stressful circumstances."

"Thank you," Kim said to me. Then she shot Brandon a dark look.

"You're welcome. If you need anything else, just let Lamont know." I nodded at Lamont.

Lamont nodded back.

From her tone, I suspected Kim was pissed enough that she'd continue the ass chewing once my friends and I left. Mike and Alyssa followed me out to the car. Lamont stayed behind.

Mike looked at me. "Are you okay?"

Alyssa touched my arm.

"I'm fine. I'm going to take Alyssa home and then I'll meet you back at the house. I have guest gift bags to work on. This ball isn't going to throw itself."

Mike shook his head. "Life with you is never boring, gorgeous."

Alyssa laughed.

"Just another day, and a perfect example of what happens when perfectly good angels go bad."

He playfully grabbed me and kissed me full on the lips. "I'll stop and pick up dinner."

I pulled away and started toward the car. "Some orange chicken would be delicious."

"Bring your minion," he pointed at Alyssa, who was getting in the car.

"Oh good. Sesame chicken for me, please." Alyssa flashed him a cheerleader smile.

I got into the car and buckled my seat belt, and watched Mike get into his car. "Wanna help make Belial Talismans?"

Alyssa nodded. "Yeah. Maybe I'll just stay the night if you don't mind. It's Saturday tomorrow anyway and Gabe is down in *the Springs* for the night."

With that, we pulled away from the curb and headed toward me and Mike's place, our heads filled with grandiose ideas for our Solstice Ball.

FINIS

About the Author

Audrey Brice is the pseudonym of a renowned Daemonolatress and practicing magician who has been performing her arts since the mid-eighties. She lives with her husband and several cats along the front range of the beautiful Rocky Mountains.

Also by Audrey Brice

Outer Darkness (OTS 1)

When socialite Chloe Brigid is murdered and the crime seems to have occult overtones, outed daemon worshiper Senator Steve Mitchell is arrested. It's up to magician Elizabeth Tanner, the public figurehead of the Ordo Templi Serpentis, to find out who outed the senator and who killed Chloe Brigid before the senator is falsely accused of the crime and The Order is investigated. What she finds, however, is not what she expects. The killer's attention soon turns toward her. Will she be able to help the police find the killer before she becomes the next victim?

Into Darkness (OTS 2)

Magus Elizabeth Tanner has been gifted some cursed magickal items. While trying to break the curse, she and her boyfriend Michael become suspects in a murder they didn't commit. To clear their names they must find the real killer by delving into a dark bdsm underworld where sex magick and the Daemonic meet. Will they be able to find a killer, clear their names, and escape their descent into darkness?

Rising Darkness (OTS 3)

Amid the glamour and lights of Hollywood, Elizabeth Tanner and her companions are back, this time investigating paranormal activity in the Beverly Hills mansion of famed actress, Kylie Ramone. The estate's haunted, dark history is the reason the Daemon worshiping starlet bought the property to begin with. When their investigations uncover an underground temple where the spirit of a dead Satanic priest demands sacrifice, Liz and her friends find themselves lingering on the precipice of an open portal to the other side.

In a dangerous battle between the living and the dead, can Liz and her friends summon a Daemonic force powerful enough to destroy the rising darkness and save Kylie Ramone's life?

Ascending Darkness (OTS 4)

The biggest name in occult television is dead. When Lucien Groner, head of the Black Magick Network, is found ritually murdered in his Parker home, the police contact magus Elizabeth Tanner to help decipher the macabre crime scene. Meanwhile, the OTS High Council instructs her to keep the Order's reputation clean, but Liz has more pressing problems of her own. Not only is she in hot water with her boss, but Mike's mother doesn't like her. She and Mike's future together hangs in the balance, and Denver's entire magickal community is on the verge of mayhem. This time, it's up to Liz to solve another murder and avert chaos before the body count rises.

The Thirteen Covens Saga

More than sixty years ago, a single coven rife with discord and mistrust shattered, leaving ruined lives in its wake. Its dedicated members forced to go their separate ways only to manifest as thirteen distinct covens, each with their own secrets to bear. Now, among the quiet country roads and still forests of upstate New York, a great evil is awakening and the covens may have no choice but to come together again. Are you ready to choose a side?

A Rising Damp
Temple Apophis
Lucifer's Haven

Other Tales:
The Danbury Ghost
Samuel

Forthcoming:
Illuminated Darkness
More Thirteen Covens!!

By Audrey Brice as Anne O'Connell

Training Amy

When Amy starts her new job at a book shop she has no idea what kind of merchandise her two bosses have stored in a private back room for select customers. She's never been allowed back there. One night, when she's closing shop alone she decides to take a look. Big mistake. Brad and Eric (her bosses) catch her snooping around. They don't tolerate rule-breakers and Amy must be punished. Will her secret desires plunge her deeper into their world? Or will she run back to the safety of her normal life and the dull boyfriend who has a dark side of his own?

Publisher's Note: This book contains explicit sexual content, graphic language, and situations that some readers may find objectionable: BDSM theme and content includes: dubious consent, bondage, spanking, toys, anal play, and menage m/f/m and m/f/f.

Other Titles:

Switched
Black Lily
Her Demon Lover
Her Demon Wedding
Domme X
The Rite
DOM 359
Weekend Captive
Sincerely, Megan
Nice Girls Don't
My Neighbor Enslaved

By Audrey Brice as S. J. Reisner

Left Horse Black

For centuries, the zealot Kersian sorcerers have abducted innocent women and children for sacrifice to their 'no name' god, and have waged war upon Danaria's sorcerers. Now, they are covertly usurping the thrones of human-ruled kingdoms to do the unthinkable; they are building a massive human army to assist them in destroying Danaria's sorcerer bloodlines in an attempt to save their own. Armed with nothing more than meager weapons, untrained sorcery, and mere instinct, a troubled human prince, an inept Danarian sorceress, and their friends, rise up and become the world's last hope to stop the Kersians, and save the sorcerers' dying race. Will they succeed?

Other Titles:
Warrior's Blood Red
Saving Sarah May

Forthcoming:
Eagle's Talon Gray
Seeress of Prylyn